SILENT EMPOWERMENT
OF THE COMPATRIOTS

Gabriel Ruhumbika

Translation from Kiswahili by the author

E&D Vision Publishing
Dar es Salaam

E & D Vision Publishing Limited
P.O.Box. 4460,
Dar es Salaam,
Tanzania.
E-mail: info@edvisionpublishing.co.tz
Web: www.edvisionpublishing.co.tz

Silent Empowerment of the Compatriots.

First published in 1992 as *Miradi Bubu ya Wazalendo* by Economic Research Bureau (ERB), University of Dar es Salaam; second edition in 1995 by Tanzania Publishing House (TPH).

ISBN: 978-9987-521-59-3

PART I
Mzee Jabiri

1

*N*dugu[1] Saidi used to tell his children that his father was Mzee[2]Jabiri son of Saidi, and that they were Wamakua from Msangusangu in West Masasi. He told them that their clan was once big and famous, but that the Almighty God has a different destiny for every human being, and had destined his own father to a life of loneliness and suffering in this world. And his one and only wish for all his children, male and female, was, God willing, for them to grow up well, and become adult men and women of good behavior. And, as soon as they became grown-ups, to marry and, with God's blessing, have many children, so as to revive their grandparents' great clan.

And indeed life in this world hadn't been kind to Ndugu Said and his late father. When Mzee Jabiri was still a young man he married as many as five wives, all of whom bore him children. But each time a wife of his gave birth, the child died. And when that wife left him and got married to another man, the children she had with that other husband of hers all lived and grew up. As a result all his wives ended by deserting him, and Mzee Jabiri lived without a single wife for a long time.

Saidi was a son born to him in his old age. He married his mother when his head was already all white with grey hair, and after he had lived for ages without marrying again. A fellow old man from their Msangusangu village had taken pity on him on seeing an adult man so good and wise like Mzee Jabiri on the verge of going to his grave without leaving an heir in this world and had given him in marriage a young daughter of his who had just reached her puberty. In no time the young girl had two children with Mzee Jabiri, Saidi first, followed by his baby sister Amina. And this time the Almighty God willed his children to live and grow up. Mzee Jabiri began counting himself a human being like others in this world! *Alhamdulillahi!*[3] But apparently that was only wishful thinking, for in no time a terrible disease fell on his family.

It was the year in which the Second World War had just ended. And the disease which wiped out the relatives of Mzee Jabiri gave a person a bit of diarrhea for one day and the following day he or she was dead. The disease first killed his father, Mzee Saidi, his dear parent who, in spite of his advanced age, was still in very good heath and living just fine independently. Then it fell on all his remaining relatives, paternal and maternal, and killed each and every one of them within a single week! And right away it fell on the relatives of his wife in the same neighborhood, killing all his in-laws, men and women, from children to adults! Two big clans of Msangusangu disappeared from the earth in a single stroke as if they had never existed! While all that was happening to him, the rest of the people in the village remained perfectly healthy! And before Mzee Jabiri knew what to do or where to go for help, his daughter Amina too followed her relatives in the land of the dead! Three days after burying his daughter, his beloved wife Idaya, the young daughter of Mwene Sefu, his friend who had saved him from dying without issue, his dear wife who brought him the incomparable blessings of being a parent, also died!

Mzee Jabiri didn't even wait for his dead wife's period of mourning[4] to end. As soon as he buried her, he held his son by the arm and turned his back on the graves of his wife and daughter and all his relatives with a solemn oath never to set foot in Masasi again.

Following the end of the Second World War, Wamakonde people from Mozambique were passing through Masasi and surrounding areas in large numbers, fleeing from the cruel rule of their Portuguese colonial masters and heading for the sisal plantations of Morogoro, Kilosa, Korogwe, Mombo and Tanga in neighboring British Tanganyika in search of work as migrant laborers. Mzee Jabiri decided to join those Wamakonde refugees and headed for the white men's migrant labor camps in distant lands he considered far enough from Masasi which had taken from him all his relatives on earth and where he hoped to find work and earn something with which to start a new life in whatever place he would end.

2

That was how Mzee Jabiri and his son Saidi, at that time about ten years of age, found themselves in Tanga, at the sisal plantation of a Greek white man known to his laborers as Bwana[5] Tumbo Tumbo[6]. But in Tanga too Mzee Jabiri and his son were in no time victims of yet another calamity.

The Mmakua old man and his son had been working as migrant laborers for the Greek Tumbo Tumbo for about a year. It was on a Saturday, at about eleven in the morning. Father and son were now both expert sisal cutters. At first it was only Mzee Jabiri who had to fill a daily quota of sisal leaves, with his son helping him. But within less than three months Saidi surprised all the laborers on the plantation, including his own father, by him too managing to cut enough sisal to fill his own daily quota! Mnyapara Mkuu[7] of the plantation, who had been nicknamed Munubi[8] by his fellow laborers on the farm, had therefore no choice but to assign that young child of ten a daily obligatory measure of sisal leaves to cut. There were people on the plantation who accused Mzee Jabiri of being an avaricious old man who loved money so much he had no pity for his own child still so young. Mzee Jabiri's answer from the bottom of his heart for such accusations was, "Let him work! If he is capable of doing this backbreaking work at such a tender age, then this is a man who will go far." For the truth was that Mzee Jabiri had no love of any kind for the sisal money. He became a laborer at the farm out of dire necessity, to try and find the means of starting a new life, after a cruel world uprooted him from his Masasi homeland without mercy. And his desire was, as soon as he put aside a bit of money, to look for a place to call home again and settle and take his child Saidi to school so that he can continue with his education. When they left their native Masasi he was already in the third grade at Msangusangu Christian Mission school, in spite of his being a Moslem, and his teachers were praising him for being intelligent in class. And Mzee Jabiri's wish was for his son to get all the education he could get.

Even though now Saidi too had his own daily quota of sisal to cut, still the chief *mnyapara* made sure he was all the time working next to his father, so that other laborers wouldn't rob him of his sisal. Where he was working beside his son, Mzee Jabiri had just finished cutting leaves from a sisal plant and on moving to the next he didn't pay attention to a pile of sisal leaves on the ground and stepped on them and slipped, fell and landed on an iron peg erect in the ground like a spear purposely put there by some enemy of his who knew he was going to fall down on that spot. All of a sudden the hundreds of laborers scattered all over the sisal farm were startled from their backbreaking toil of cutting and heaving sisal leaves by a single shout of "Aaaa!", followed by loud cries of "Father! Father! Fatheeer!..."

The first person to arrive at the scene was Mnyapara Munubi. Munubi was his fellow laborers' nickname for him, and the only name of his they knew. No one knew his real name. At the same time, nobody dared call him by that nickname. The name they called him by when he was present was Mnyapara Mkuu, his title, because Munubi signified his fellow laborers' hatred for him. He was a Mmakonde like the majority of the laborers on that sisal plantation but, because of his cruelty, everybody decided he was "Mkosakabila,"[9] a person of no known origin, who knew no human fellowship. And because he was unusually black, they decided he must be a Nubian from far off Sudan. And Mnyapara Munubi wasn't only cruel. He was also terrifying: almost seven feet tall, with arms as big as tree logs and a swollen chest like a rhinoceros! It was said that Bwana Tumbo Tumbo gave him the job of Mnyapara Mkuu right away on the very day he set foot on his plantation to look for camp labor, on account of his terrifying physique.

On seeing the accident his laborer had, Munubi reprimanded Saidi sharply, "A grown man, you see your father wounded and all you do is to holler! Quick, go to the camp and bring a bedsheet, at once!" Saidi took off running to their living quarters while trembling from head to foot. Now people were arriving at the scene of the accident from everywhere, holding in their hands their machetes for cutting sisal and stones and big sticks they had picked up on the way. When they heard Mzee Jabiri's cry piercing the sky everyone concluded it was one of them who that day again had been bitten by a snake, their greatest danger at their work of cutting sisal leaves in farms overgrown with thickets and tall grass.

Munubi did not answer a single one of the endless questions thrown at him from every side: "What is it, Mnyapara Mkuu? "What on earth happened? "What happened to Mzee Jabiri!..." By now Mzee Jabiri way lying on the ground completely still. The only thing which showed he was still alive was blood gushing out of his left eye. The iron peg on which he fell had pierced his eye all the way to the skull. Without uttering a single word, Mnyapara Munubi knelt down and grabbed a handful of soil from the ground. The soil was still wet from the heavy rains of the previous night and he mixed the wet soil with the blood from Mzee Jabiri's wound. He then kneaded the blood-soaked mud into Mzee Jabiri's wounded eye until he completely sealed the awful hole. Then, still without saying a word, he ripped with his hands a leaf from a sisal plant nearby and tore off a big strip with his teeth and began chewing the sisal. In the meanwhile all around him his laborers were gazing at him in complete disbelief. When he took the chewed sisal from his mouth he put it on top of the mud with which he had sealed the hole in Mzee Jabiri's eye. And that was when he really surprised everybody there. In those days the plantation laborers' uniform consisted of a shirt and a pair of shorts or a bedsheet wrapped around the waist. Mnyapara Munubi, as the chief foreman of the plantation, wore around his waist a proper *kikoi* loin cloth instead of an ordinary bedsheet the rank and file laborers wore. After putting on Mzee Jabiri's wound the sisal he had ground with his teeth, he took off his loin cloth and remained as naked as he was born, since in those days men hadn't began wearing underpants beneath their outer clothes. He then shredded his entire *kikoi* into bandages for dressing Mzee Jabiri's wound. It wasn't until he had dressed the man's wound nicely that he looked up and glanced around and found Saidi had returned and was holding a bedsheet in his hands and took the bedsheet and wrapped it around his waist and covered his nakedness again. Then he lifted the wounded man from the ground and carried him and made for the camp. Mzee Jabiri too, in spite of his age, was a tall man of heavy built, but still Mnyapara Mkuu easily carried him in his arms as if he were an infant! He continued to surprise his laborers by taking the injured man to his chief foreman's living quarters instead of his laborer's shack. Ordinary laborers slept on bare wooden planks laid on the floor with no beddings of any kind. It was only Mnyapara Mkuu who had a bed with a mattress in his living quarters. On arriving at his place he laid the old man on his bed.

Since it was on a Saturday, Bwana Tumbo Tumbo was in the city of Tanga, with its big hotels and private clubs, eating, getting drunk and enjoying life with his fellow rich whites. And usually he didn't come back until Monday morning. There was no medical aid of any kind in the plantation camp, not even medicine for dressing wounds, in spite of the fact that sisal laborers injured themselves badly with their machetes and on the sisal-leaf thorns all the time at work. And during those days once a man was hired as a camp laborer on a sisal plantation, sisal being the leading cash crop of the colonial economy of the British masters of Tanganyika, he was the prisoner of the foreign owner of the plantation until the end of his contract, of two, three or even four years. It did not matter whether he had been conscripted on the orders of his District Officer for failing to pay capital tax or for some felony he had been accused of or whether he had gone to look for work of his own accord due to some pressing needs of his like Mzee Jabiri and his son, once enrolled as a camp laborer that person was under the rule of his employer day and night until the end of his contract period. And a plantation laborer was obliged to live in the farm camp, had no permission to receive visitors, not even his wife, and could not travel beyond the confines of his employer's farm without the permission of his employer. Mzee Jabiri could not therefore be taken to hospital until his employer returned from enjoying himself, since it was strictly forbidden to go and call him home, even if the life of a person depended on it.

Saidi and Mnyapara Munubi stayed by the bedside of the wounded man all the time for the two days they waited for the return of Bwana Tumbo Tumbo, without any one of them leaving to go anywhere even for a single minute. Saidi, a young boy who had already witnessed his mother, his sister, and the rest of his relatives all suddenly die, was shaken to the core of his being by the calamity which had befallen his father, except he did not cry and had not cried again since Mnyapara Munubi reprimanded him. Mzee Jabiri himself hadn't uttered a word since his accident, on account of the pain together with the thoughts consuming his mind. He asked himself what he had done wrong for the Almighty God to rain calamities on him so relentlessly! Above all he asked himself what would become of his young child with no other relative in this world besides himself should that accident be the way his Creator had prescribed for him to join his relatives where they had all disappeared to within a single day! Mnyapara Munubi on his part all he thought of was how the wounded man was doing: "If this fever relents, he will recover. He will be blind in one eye, but he will recover," he kept on repeating to himself. By nighttime Mzee Jabiri had such a high fever that he was frantically rolling and tossing in bed all the time.

The first signs of the injured man getting better were seen at eight o'clock on Sunday morning. Mzee Jabiri fell asleep for a fairly long time and then woke up with a start, dripping with sweat, and at once spoke: "Could I have a bit of water to drink?" And after drinking some water he fell asleep again. Munubi touched him on the forehead and found his fever had cooled. And this time he slept for a long time and peacefully. Munubi became hopeful: "If he continues this way, he has recovered," he said to himself again.

Mzee Jabiri did not wake up again until the middle of the night: "Is Saidi here?" On dressing his wound Mnyapara Munubi had wrapped bandages over both his eyes and he therefore could not see. "He is here, Mzee," Mnyapara Munubi answered. Had his laborers been around they would have been even more amazed, because their Mnyapara Mkuu they knew did not have the humanity to address anybody as "Mzee", even a person older than his father.

"Saidi, you and I your father are the unfortunate ones of the world," Mzee Jabiri said, in a weak but clearly audible voice. "My son, now listen to me," he continued without giving his son time to say anything. "When a person falls sick, it means two things. There is getting well again, but there is also not recovering. So if for me not recovering is what the Almighty God has willed, know well that you will be left all alone in this world. It will be left to you to save from extinction your grandparents clans, the clan of your paternal grandfather, your namesake Mzee Saidi, and that of your maternal grandfather, the father of your dear mother, the daughter of Mwene[10] Sefu, may God rest her soul in peace. May it therefore please God to

---
10

take good care of you, and may you, in spite of your heavy lot, grow up into an adult of good behavior. Then get married, and may Providence continue to bless you and give you children, and may God will them many, who you will nurture into good adults like you. To a human being there is no better fortune than that in this world." With that Mzee Jabiri said no more and silently listened to his pain and unbearable thoughts.

Saidi once more felt tears threatening to drop from his eyes for the second time but remembered the reprimand at the scene of the accident by Mnyapara Mkuu, the one person who was with him every minute since his Mzee's injury, and held back his tears and just answered back his father with, "Yes, Mzee."

As soon as it dawned on Monday, Mnyapara Munubi made very thin gruel for the injured man, and Mzee Jabiri managed to sit up on the bed and drink a bit of it. On seeing that, his two sickbed attendants felt a bit reassured and just waited for the return of Bwana Tumbo Tumbo so that their patient could be taken to the hospital.

3

*B*wana Tumbo Tumbo's house was about a quarter of a mile from the laborers camp. It was a large white house with a red-tile roof standing on a small hill and surrounded by pine trees in the midst of a well-tendered lawn watered daily and its short grass always carefully trimmed as if a barber had given it a hair cut. The plantation workshop was by the camp, the laborers living quarters, with Bwana Tumbo Tumbo's office adjoining the workshop. A tarmac road running strait as an arrow between two rows of pine trees was the way by which the plantation owner descended from his home on the top of the hill to his office, so that someone standing at his office or at the workshop could see all the way to his master's hilltop home. In the same building with Bwana Tumbo Tumbo's Office was the Laborers Office, where the farm hands went to receive their weekly ration of corn floor, bean and salt, the only fare laborers lived on daily all over the sisal plantations in the country, and where a laborer who had broken the master's regulations went to receive strokes of the cane administered by the cruel giant Mnyapara Munubi under the supervision of Bwana Tumbo Tumbo himself. That too was where a farm hand in need of anything went to face the boss. That morning, after Munubi gave the wounded man gruel, he at once moved him to his laborer's shack in the camp, so that when Bwana Tumbo Tumbo returned he wouldn't be in trouble for breach of discipline and serious violation of plantation rules by daring to lodge an ordinary laborer in his Mnyapara Mkuu's hut! He then left Mzee Jabiri in the care of his son Saidi and went to the laborers office to wait for their boss.

It was not until half past eight that Mnyapara Mkuu spotted Bwana Tumbo Tumbo's car arriving on the hilltop. He braced himself for another period of waiting, of at least two hours, because he knew that before coming to work his boss had first to take a bath, change clothes, and then attend to the most important daily work of his life: eating. Bwana Tumbo Tumbo lived without a wife or children in his home, claiming they were in his country in Europe, but what his laborers knew for sure about their master was that his wife and children and his God was his stomach. Every cook and houseboy who ever worked in his home was amazed at how that white man adored food! On waking up, before leaving his bed or brushing his teeth, he had first to be served a whole kettle of coffee with milk. When he finished taking a bath he started off his breakfast with a plateful of fruits, then a glass of fruit juice, to which he added a bowlful of gruel made with milk, before going on to attack first a plate of bacon, followed by boiled eggs, then fried eggs served with fried cow kidney and liver together with fried potatoes, beans and chutney. And then he concluded with bread with butter and jam, which he watered down with another kettle of coffee with milk! And that was just the beginning. At lunchtime a huge table capable of sitting twelve people was full of food for him alone, which he ate and cleaned off completely! And that wasn't the end. His dinner at night was the real feast! Daily! The result being what turned him into Master Tumbo Tumbo, a creature so fat that his hands couldn't reach the back of his body, and as a consequence he subjected his workers to disgusting and demeaning drudgery as if they weren't his fellow human beings! He took a bath by his houseboys first soaping and cleaning his back and then hosing him down as if they were washing a hog. And every time he went to relieve himself one of his houseboys had to follow him into the toilet and, when he finished shitting all over his body the rot and stench of his greed of a hyena, that servant of his wiped and washed his behind clean of his shit!

That morning Bwana Tumbo Tumbo got into his office at eleven sharp. He was busy attending to matters of his office and the workshop for one whole hour, and it wasn't until one o'clock when he finally moved on to the laborers office, where his Mnyapara Mkuu was still waiting for him, since it was strictly forbidden for anybody to see him for anything except in that office reserved for his laborers problems. He had already changed from his holiday best, in which he enjoyed life with his fellow Europeans during weekends, into his work clothes: a khaki safari jacket and khaki pair of shorts and a bowl-shaped helmet hard like iron, also khaki in color. From a distance it was difficult for a person to tell his front from his back, since he was all swollen and round like an overaged pig. He was still some distance away when Mnyapara Munubi was overwhelmed by a very strong smell of some disgusting perfume and heard the breathing of a hippopotamus and knew his employer was coming.

A laborer who fell sick and couldn't go to work wouldn't be paid that day, since he had not filled his daily quota of sisal leaves, and the one who was so sick that most likely he wouldn't be able to go back to work soon would normally be fired. So when Mnyapara Munubi told his employer of Mzee Jabiri's accident, emphasizing that it was a very bad one, Bwna Tumbo Tumbo's answer was, "Count total of his quota and report to office. I pay him and matter finished." But it appeared this time Mnyapara Munubi was determined to surprise not only his fellow laborers but their master himself as well, because he did not answer with, "Yes, Master," and salute and go and do his master's bidding as he was wont to. And by not doing so he indeed surprised and really angered him! There and then his eyes turned red and bulged out and his hair stood up on his head like the quills of a porcupine!

"Nyapara Kuu!" he shouted so loud you would think the person he was talking to was in a distant building instead of standing beside him.

"Yes, Master."

"You not hear my order?"

"I heard, Master."

"How you still standing here!"

"There is a problem, Master. The laborer injured is a bit different from the other laborers…"

"What you meaning is different from other laborers!" his master cut him short. Whenever he was angry his neck swelled like that of a cobra and he breathed not like one but a hundred hippopotamuses. Usually the laborer who provoked his demon that way would, poor creature, piss and sometimes even shit in his pants without knowing it. However, it appeared this time Mnyapara Munubi was ready to face even his own death, since he still found something to say to Bwana Tumbo Tumbo:

"May be it is because the accident itself was unusual, because since he was injured the workers in the entire camp talk of nothing else but his accident. Personally what I fear is that if we don't take him to the hospital to get treated and he dies there may be trouble. The laborers may go on strike. And you too, Master, know the problems a strike causes." That was what Mnyapara Munubi's mind invented as an answer to his master.

From time to time, sisal plantation laborers went on strike. From tie to time, the foreign owners of the farms, out of their greed for profit and because they did not consider a black person a human being like themselves, overworked their laborers and treated them so badly that they couldn't take it anymore and went on strike. But most of the times those strikes were quickly and easily put down. The plantation owner went to Tanga or Morogoro or Dar es Salaam and came back escorted by policemen with guns and canes and handcuffs, and at once the policemen's canes went to work and the leaders of the strike and stubborn workers were thrown in jail and the rest were made to behave and went back to work, with their share of punishment to boot, cuts in wages and food rations for a long period to make sure in the future they would think twice before daring to go on strike again. In spite of that, laborers strikes were an unwelcome problem to plantation owners. It was still true that a strike, however short lived, meant that work on the farm and in the workshop stopped and caused a loss of revenue. What was more, there had been cases where the laborers refused to give in, in spite of the drastic measures taken against them by the Government, and as a result the strikes lasted a long time and caused irremediable losses to the business owners. There was therefore no sisal plantation owner in his proper mind who did not secretly dread strikes, however much he may pretend not to care. Bwana Tumbo Tumbo too, on hearing his Mnyapara Mkuu, the one person on whom he counted to make everybody on his farm behave, warning him that way, decided it was in his interest to listen to him. The nearest hospital was some fifteen miles from Bwana Tumbo Tumbo's plantation and belonged to English missionaries. It was a paying hospital, and when a farm owner's laborers were treated there their employer paid and then deducted the amount from their wages. Bwana Tumbo Tumbo always took his sick laborers to the hospital personally, to make sure they got treated at once and those not too sick returned to work without loss of time. His saloon car was exclusively for his personal use. He therefore took one of the trucks for carrying sisal and Mnyapara Mkuu jumped at the back and they went to Mzee Jabiri's shack to take him to the hospital.

Mzee Jabiri now appeared out of danger and his condition no longer worrying. Mnyapara Mkuu's treatment had worked fairly well. When they went to fetch him, he thanked his Mnyapara Mkuu for everything he had done for him, speaking quiet cheerfully. But all the same he was still too sick to seat alone at the back of a truck without someone supporting him. Bwana Tumbo Tumbo never allowed a laborer to sit with the driver in the truck cabin, even when he wasn't the driver. He therefore allowed Munubi and Saidi to sit with the injured man behind the truck and accompany him to the hospital.

The truck was open at the back. Mnyapara Munubi was sitting with his legs spread out on the floor of the truck with his back resting on the truck cabin, cradling on his lap the head of the patient who lay on his back between his legs. Said was seated besides him, likewise with his back against the truck cabin. They had not covered a mile when Mnyapara Munubi was already regretting why he had even asked that Mzee Jabiri be taken to the hospital. This time Bwana Tumbo Tumbo wasn't just driving fast so as to arrive quickly and return as soon as possible. He was driving like someone who had been forced to make the trip and wanted to make Mnyapara Mkuu and his patient pay for their insolence. From the time they got on the road, they were being tossed about this way and that way. In no time Munubi and Saidi heard their patient moaning. And shortly after that they saw blood ooze out of the bandages on his wound, for the first time since Munubi dressed it after the accident. Mnyapara Munubi did not know what to do. His master wasn't a person to whom one could appeal to reduce the speed at which he had chosen to drive. All he could do therefore was to turn to the wounded man and console him: "Mzee Jabiri, just have patience, my old man. The hospital is not far, we will get there right now."

Traveling on the back of a goods truck on those terrible roads, even at a reasonable speed, was never a comfortable journey, even for someone who isn't sick. The road was nothing but ditches and gaping holes, from beginning to end. And that was where the injured person was being driven as if they were flying in an airplane! Suddenly Munubi and Saidi together with their patient found themselves tossed

17

high up in the air. The truck had plunged into a large hole in the middle of the road. When they landed back on the truck, Munubi and Saidi fell on one side and the sick man on the other. And before Munubi had managed to get hold of the patient and cradle him again, they were thrown in the air a second time, this time more violently and really high up! When they settled back a bit and Mnyapara Munubi and Saidi managed to hold and support their patient again, Munubi realized that Mzee Jabiri had fainted. On looking at him more carefully, he saw that he was bleeding from a new wound, at the back of his head. Apparently, when Mzee Jabiri was tossed in the air on falling down his head hit a heavy piece of iron nearby. In spite of knowing fully well that his master never allowed anybody to talk to him without asking for his permission first, Mnyapara Mkuu found himself repeatedly knocking on top of the cabin of the truck for his master to stop. But, on hearing that, his white master, without even bothering to find out what was the matter, now drove like a real madman!

When they arrived at the hospital he stopped the truck by breaking violently and noisily and setting off a cloud of dust. Then he got out of the truck by slamming the door so loudly you would think a bomb had exploded, at the same time shouting at the top of his voice and breathing while panting and snorting, his neck already all swollen, saliva and insults spouting out of his mouth, "All right, put down your laborer quick and explain why you make your stupid noises to me! Damn you, savage!..."

Fortunately his truck had made so much noise on stopping that the entire hospital had been startled and people came out to see what was happening, among them Sister Superior, the head of the white religious sisters who were running the hospital, and the presence of a white woman on the scene somehow turned Mnyapara Munubi's white master too into a human being instead of a mad buffalo without pity or shame and saved the head foreman from more insults and further trouble.

They arrived at the hospital at about two in the afternoon. Only Bwana Tumbo Tumbo and the white Sister accompanied the nurses carrying the wounded man on a stretcher into the hospital. Saidi and Munubi were forbidden to go inside. Until six there was no sign of Bwana Tumbo Tumbo coming out of the hospital. When he finally emerged, accompanied by the white religious woman, it was already dark. On his stretcher, Mzee Jabiri was now covered from head to foot with the bedsheet he came to the hospital wearing with his laborer's shirt. There was therefore no need for anybody to ask what had happened. Even the young child Saidi realized beyond doubt that his father was no longer among the living. It was Sister Superior in charge of the hospital who felt there was need to say something.

"You late bring your patient here, you see! He bleeding a lot of blood inside his head when his eye got accident. Blood bleeding his inside is what killed him, understand? And much dirt your people put inside his eye also made his sickness more, you hear? Tell your people, you see!" The Sister was saying all that while holding Saidi by the shoulders, her eyes peering deep into his eyes as if she was a fortune-teller reading signs in the boy's eyes, no doubt because Bwana Tumbo Tumbo had told her he was the deceased laborer's son. Hospital nurses had already put his father's body on the truck which had brought them. Munubi decided to save Saidi from the iron grip of the white woman's hands by getting hold of his hand and climbing with him onto the back of the truck besides his father's body.

As usual, the laborers' living shacks were scattered with pit latrines. Because the latrines were also used as bathrooms, their holes did not take long to fill. In Bwana Tumbo Tumbo's plantation there was an area right at the edge of the farm set aside for burying the waste emptied from those latrine pits whenever they were full. Those huge holes for burying feces in Bwana Tumbo Tumbo's farm were also the graves where laborers who died in his camp were buried. It was into one of those holes full of excrement that Mnyapara Munubi and the young child of the deceased, Saidi, that night on getting back to the farm threw the body of Mzee Jabiri, under the supervision of Bwana Tumbo Tumbo, who was shouting at them and telling them to hurry up, "Quick, quick, throw away your dirt of your dead man! Because of you, me already late for my dinner!"

When it dawned the following day, Bwana Tumbo Tumbo woke up to find the number of laborers on his farm diminished, and not only because Mzee Jabiri had died. His Mnyapara Mkuu, Munubi, as well as the young son of the deceased, Saidi, had both found out that the plantation of that white master was no place for a human being to live.

PART II

Mnyapara Munubi

4

To the laborers of Bwana Tumbo Tumbo's plantation, their Mnyapara Mkuu they knew and the man they decided to call Munubi was a cruel brute without pity, just like their white master, a dirty bastard who treated his fellow human beings worse than dogs. It never occurred to a single one of them that perhaps Mnyapara Munubi was doing that work of brutalizing his fellow laborers out of necessity, just as they had to continue working for that bastard of a master. Therefore nobody could understand what he did for the deceased, Mzee Jabiri, from the time of his accident until he died, or why he would run away from his work, from his friend Bwana Tumbo Tumbo, his fellow brutal bastard, and take the child of the dead man with him.

The truth of the matter however was that with Mnyapara Munubi too it was necessity which brought him all the way from his native Mozambique to Bwana Tumbo Tumbo's plantation. He was an orphan, and an only child whose father and mother died when he was still an infant. He did not even know how they looked like. He was brought up by some distant relatives of his parents. Life in that colony of the Portuguese whites was so difficult that he had to stop attending school when he was in third grade and begin working and trying to be independent so as to help his relatives who were raising him make ends meet. He too had therefore started working on the plantations of foreign white settlers when he was ten years of age, the age at which Saidi, the son of the dead man, started working at Bwana Tumbo Tumbo's farm, with the difference that with him at that age he looked like a boy of fifteen or older. At the age of nineteen he looked a fully grown up man and was already Mnyapara Mkuu on a large farm of a Portuguese cashewnut grower. It was at that farm that he got into trouble.

As Mnyapara Mkuu, he reported to the plantation works clerk, a young Portuguese man of about twenty-five years of age. One day his supervisor was not satisfied with his work and shouted, hurling insults at him, all the way to insulting his mother. On hearing the man insult his mother, who left him in this world before he even knew how she looked like, Mnyapara Mkuu was so overwhelmed with anger his head felt as if it would explode! But he feared for his job, and the person who had insulted him was white, and so he bottled it all inside him and said nothing. Unfortunately the young white man, on seeing that he could insult, as he wanted, that elephant of a man without the giant daring to even say a single word, thought he could do with him whatever he pleased and began slapping and kicking him. This time Mnyapara Mkuu answered, by hitting the young Portuguese man in the middle of the chest once with a fist. The white young man dropped to the ground like a sack of sand and fainted. He was carried to the hospital on a stretcher.

Mnyapara Munubi did not need to be told by anybody that for him Mozambique was no longer a country in which he could live. During those colonial days, an African to strike a white person meant risking a long period in jail, if not death by hanging, irrespective of whether the unfortunate black person was provoked or acted in self defense. He first ran to Mtwara and hid among his fellow Wamakonde on the British Tanganyika side of the border. He had not been in Mtwara for even one month when he heard that the European man he fought with, who was still in the hospital all those days, had died from pain in his chest. Mtwara, so close to Mozambique, was no place for him anymore. That was why he pushed on farther away until he arrived in Tanga, at Bwana Tumbo Tumbo's, looking for sisal plantation work, and was at once given his usual job of Mnyapara Mkuu.

Running away from his master Bwana Tumbo Tumbo's plantation that night wasn't something he had planned, or even thought about for a long time. It was just the events of that day, starting with their trip to the hospital and the brutal murder of their old man by that white man, and then him and the son of the dead man being forced to commit the abomination of throwing the body of their dead old man in a pit of excrement, which pained him and filled him with so much anger that he told himself he had to leave that place at once. "Otherwise I am bound to kill this abominable white man. And this time I will have nowhere to hide. And no one should be hanged for killing such a bastard," he told himself.

He was seated with the son of the dead laborer in his Mnyapara Mkuu's hut, having just come from the shit pit where they had dumped the body of their dead old man as if it were the carcass of a dog! None of them had uttered a single word since they left the hospital with the body of their dead. When Mnyapara Mkuu made that decision, he turned and faced the dead man's son and told him, "This is not a place for a human being to live. You too witnessed how this white man killed your father, regardless of how the white woman at the hospital tried to insult our intelligence, no doubt because to white people a black person is a baboon with no intelligence. And now look at the abomination we have just committed at his orders! Get your belongings, we are leaving."

Five hours on foot from Bwana Tumbo Tumbo's farm in the direction of Mombo, there was a sisal plantation whose Mnyapara Mkuu was a relative of Munubi and one of the men with whom he had traveled from Mtwara to Tanga in search of migrant work. That was where Munubi and Saidi fled to that night. That same night Mnyapara Munubi entrusted Saidi in the care of his relative and asked him to hide the boy until he had arranged for him to go to Dar es Salaam and found a person to receive him there. Then Munubi himself, that same night, disappeared again into the darkness of endless sisal plantations.

5

*M*unubi got his second labor-camp job near the town of Morogoro, on the sisal plantation of a South African Boer called George. This time he was determined to work as just an ordinary laborer, but at that farm too he was given his usual job of Mnyapara Mkuu, and the laborer who was the head foreman was demoted by Boer George and made his assistant, and Munubi had no option but to accept the job. He had worked for white people long enough to know that, since he found work with another white man, even if Bwana Tumbo Tumbo looked for him and found him he couldn't set the police on him and have him thrown in jail for absconding from his employer's labor camp before the end of his contract.

Boer George was not a dirty and abominable creature like Bwana Tumbo Tumbo, even though when it came to being strict and brutal it was difficult to choose between those two white masters. At Boer George's plantation corporal punishment was rarely administered. That foreign employer considered that form of punishment of no benefit to him. Instead his usual punishment for a laborer who broke any of his regulations was for the culprit to receive no pay for a month or more. And his regulations were so many that it was impossible for a single day to go by without many laborers being found in breach of a number of them. And it was too bad for the laborer who got punished that way often without mending his ways! That one would then receive corporal punishment on top of the usual one of working without pay. And the whip at Boer George's plantation was punishment meant to literally kill a person! The poor creature was first stripped completely naked, and then a piece of cloth soaked in brine would be placed on his buttocks, and the strokes of the cane then administered on the naked flesh of his bare buttocks covered with a wet piece of cloth dripping with brine. And the strokes of a sjambok of real hippopotamus hide. And never less that twenty-four of them or more!

At Boer George's plantation too, whipping laborers was the job of Mnyapara Mkuu, usually the most muscular laborer on the farm. The first man Mnyapara Munubi whipped at the farm was an old laborer of about fifty years of age. He didn't even know what the man had been accused of. He was just called by his master and told to do his job.

One of the regulations at Boer George's plantation was that all the other laborers on the farm had to witness their fellow laborer receiving that brutal punishment, like spectators of a soccer match cheering their players! On seeing himself surrounded by his fellow laborers from the entire camp while gripping in his hands a huge rod of a sjambok, and while on the ground before him lay that poor weak old man, his head all white with grey hair, and as naked as he was born, his buttocks covered with a cloth soaked in brine so that the strokes of the whip would really mangle his flesh, Mnyapara Munubi stopped seeing clear. His head reeled and he felt dizzy. But when his master ordered him to give the man twenty-four strokes of the sjambok, he lifted his log of an arm up in the air and inflicted the punishment. A cry of "Aaaa!" from underneath him burst his ears! It was as if he was the one who had received that murderous stroke of a sjambok and he wanted to run away out of pain, except his legs felt paralyzed and he couldn't move.

27

"You nyapara, what you doing now! I say give twenty-four sjambok strokes, not one!" Boer George shouted really loud at him, now standing so close to his face as if he wanted to bite his nose, his saliva jetting out of his mouth into Mnyapara Munubi's mouth and all over his face. On being shouted at that way, the head foreman remembered that he was a *mnyapara* and that man his employer and that his job was to obey the master's orders, and lifted again the sjambok and continued whipping the man. He did not know whether or not the old man on the ground continued crying out, how many strokes he gave him, when he stopped whipping him, or who told him to stop. He only realized that he had stopped whipping the old man and someone was pouring a pail of water on his head and his buttocks where he dealt him the blows were covered in blood!

That night Mnyapara Munubi could not sleep. Whenever he closed his eyes and was about to fall asleep, he dreamt of himself whipping that laborer. Only now it wasn't that laborer anymore but the late Mzee Jabiri. Mzee Jabiri himself in person, his head and beard all white with grey hair, lying down there on the ground, as naked as he was born, in front of all those laborers young enough to be his children, his only dress the piece of brine-soaked cloth on his buttocks! Each time he lowered his huge arm and cut with that big hippopotamus-hide whip into the bare flesh of his buttocks soaked in brine, Mzee Jabiri screamed with the sky-rending cry he made the day he injured his eye on Bwana Tumbo Tumbo's farm! And still he continued whipping him. Each time he dealt him a blow blood gushed out and spurted until a river of blood formed on the ground! And still he continued dealing the old man blow after blow, at the same time as some laborers were pouring water on Mzee Jabiri's head to revive him and yet others were begging him to stop beating the poor old man before he killed him.

And still he kept on belaboring the old man with blows. And when he got to that point he would wake up. Every time he closed his eyes and dozed off a bit, the same dream returned, to end only when he jumped out of sleep, soaked in sweat and trembling all over. Finally, at about dawn of the first cock crow, fatigue from the endless ordeal saved him from the nightmare by plunging him into deep sleep.

Mnyapara Munubi was wakened from sound sleep by a person loudly knocking at his door: "Mnyapara Mkuu! Mnyapara Mkuu! May I come in! May I come in!..." He woke up and sat on his bed and answered, "Who is there? What do you want?"

"It is I, your boy Saidi, the son of your friend Mzee Jabiri. He is here with me. I accompanied him to come and see you. We are in the house already, in the sitting room, because we found the door unlocked, just closed shut."

With his hands trembling so much that he could hardly hold anything, Mnyapara Munubi looked for and finally found a box of matches and lit his tin-can paraffin lamp and went to the sitting room, his heart pounding as if it wanted to burst open his chest and sweating all over as if someone had poured a bucket of water over his head. And indeed in the sitting room of his Mnyapara Mkuu's hut on Boer George's farm there was Mzee Jabiri with his son Saidi, the old man seated on a chair and his son standing behind him. Saidi had his clothes on but Mzee Jabiri himself was completely naked! And that was not all. He was dripping with feces and urine from head to foot, and the filth itself was mixed with blood as if someone had first emptied a pail of excrement over his head and then poured blood over the shit! Mzee Jabiri on seeing Mnyapara Mkuu shaking all over that way addressed him, "Do not be afraid my friend, Mnyapara Mkuu. Yes, it was me you whipped with the sjambok out there today. But I know you didn't recognize me, because to Mnyapara Mkuu rank-and-file laborers all look alike. I therefore cannot blame you for not

29

recognizing me. As to whipping me, you were simply doing your job. I have come here only to look for a place where I can stay for a while until my wounds from the sjambok caning heal and I can go to look for migrant labor somewhere else. Here our employer has fired me because of fainting before I had completed my punishment. I tried to go and hide in the shacks of my fellow laborers, but everywhere I went people chased me away saying I stink of shit! The only thing left for me to do was therefore to ask your boy here, my son Saidi, to accompany me to your place, since you and him are the only persons in this world who know why I stink of shit."

In the morning that day, Boer George and his laborers woke up to find their Mnyapara Mkuu gone, without saying good-bye to anybody, or telling a soul where he was heading!

From that day on the life of Mnyapara Mkuu became that of endless wandering. Everywhere he went to look for work he was, as usual, made Mnyapara Mkuu, the job his God who created him with the body of an elephant and the awesome strength of a lion predestined him for. And everywhere he worked as Mnyapara Mkuu sooner or later a day came when he had to perform that special job of a laborer with that title, of whipping his fellow laborers on behalf of their master. And the day he performed his terrifying job at night he was paid a visit by the late Mzee Jabiri and his son Saidi, in exactly the same way as on their first visit, and saying exactly the same words to him. And the following morning the owner of that place of work and his laborers woke up to find their Mnyapara Mkuu gone, without a single soul knowing why or where he went! And that became his life year after year, until TANU[11] was born in the land and its politics finally brought *Uhuru*[12] to Tanganyika and the end of the era of the whip-wielding foreman.

6

The independence of Tanganyika found Mnyapara Munubi in Kilosa, at another sisal labor camp, after he had worked all over the country and in all sorts of white employers' labor gangs. His employer in Kilosa was an English plantation owner, and his title now was no longer Mnyapara Mkuu but Camp Headman. Since independence, calling *mwananchi*[13] *mnyapara* of an employer would have been a great insult. Also since independence, sisal plantation and work-camp laborers anywhere and everywhere in the country were free workers and no longer prisoners of their employers. In sisal farmworker-camps now people lived with their families as they pleased and, what was more, many farmworkers now lived outside the plantation camps, coming to cut sisal on the farm and returning to their homes.

In independent Tanganyika, Mnyapara Munubi was no longer some feared buffalo but a human being like others, with his own proper name by which he was called by others. And so at the Englishman's sisal plantation in Kilosa, to his fellow workers Mnyapara Munubi was Paulo, Paulo Mmakonde, or Big Paulo, for those who wanted to identify him further by the attribute of his physique. More than that he too now had friends, and many. His greatest friend among them was a fellow Mmakonde called Toma, also a farmworker at the Englishman's plantation, who lived in a community settlement not far from their employer's farm. Toma lived with his wife and children and a sister of his, a divorced woman of about thirty years of age who came to live with her brother when her marriage ended. At his friend Toma's home was the place to find Mnyapara Munubi on Saturdays and Sundays and almost everyday in the evening after work. And before long he was engaged to his friend's sister.

In all his life before that, Mnyapara Munubi had never paid much attention to women. He was torn away from his native Mozambique by his troubles when he was still too young and an orphan struggling all alone in the world to make something of his life. From there he was right away burdened by the job of Mnyapara Mkuu of an abominable master, Bwana Tumbo Tumbo, in addition to carrying with him all the time the secret of the bane which banished him from his homeland together with the fear of any time being found where he was hiding and taken back to Mozambique to be hanged. And after that his life already full of tribulations became a victim of yet another curse of being visited year in and year out by that friend of his from the land of the dead, Mzee Jabiri. Eliza, the sister of his friend, was the first woman he got to know closely enough since he too began to live the life of a normal human being. Fortunately for him, he found Eliza too ready to welcome his relationship, her anger against her husband who left her after six years of marriage in which they had three children together having cooled. Four years had passed since she came to live with her brother following her divorce, and the anger and bitterness which had made her see every man in this world as an awful creature and vow never to get married again in her life had cooled down to a point where she had began to feel a bit lonely and to desire a man in her life again, a life companion with whom to share the secrets of their hearts. And so Paulo and Eliza became a man and a woman of the same word and desire, and Toma and his wife gave them their blessings and wished them the best and they got married.

Munubi, as the Headman of the plantation camp, was living in the farmworkers barracks on the farm, in a big and fairly beautiful house. However, because of what he had been through, workers barracks on a sisal plantation was not a place where he wanted to live with his wife, notwithstanding that much had changed in almost every aspect of the lives of farmworkers since independence. Even though those workers camps were no longer virtual prisons they used to be during the colonial days, all sorts of trouble broke out in there all the time. Paulo wanted his Eliza to live in a place where nobody bothered her and one which, should God bless them with children, their children could call home. So before he got married he had, with the help of his friend Toma, obtained a plot of land in the community settlement where his friend lived. His job of Mnyapara Mkuu, much as it had soured his life, had all the same enabled him to put aside in the Post Office Savings Bank enough money for the construction at that time of a fairly good corrugated-iron roof house. And without further ado he built his home. And it was to his new home that he took his Eliza after their wedding at the Roman Catholic Church of the town of Kilosa. Both Eliza and he were Roman Catholic Christians, Mnyapara Munubi had never married before and Eliza's first marriage was a traditional one. None of them therefore had an impediment to their marriage being blessed by their church. And the priest who blessed their wedding came to bless their new house as well.

That was how Mnyapara Mkuu completed settling down in his life of a normal human being in independent Tanganyika.

Mnyapara Munubi had continued to live in his workplace house so that Eliza and he would move into their own house together, after their wedding and after the priest who would marry them had blessed it. Their wedding was on Saturday, and the following Monday when Mnyapara Munubi's employer came to work he found his Camp Headman waiting for him at his office, ready to inform him he got married and had moved to his own house and to return to him the key of his house in the farm barracks.

Even though now Tanganyika was independent and wananchi ruled their own country, still former long time underlings of colonial masters like Mnyapara Mkuu hadn't stopped saluting white people. So when his employer entered the office his Camp Headman greeted him with, "Morning, Master!" while saluting him.

"What you want, Camp Headman?" was his employer's answer to his great respect.

"Master, I have come to inform you that I got married and I have moved into my house…"

"What you saying?" his employer cut him short.

"Master, I have come to return the key of my camp house, because I will now be living outside the camp."

There were two other people in the waiting room of their employer's office who also wanted to see their boss, the farm Accountant, a long time Indian employee of the plantation who started off as a farm clerk, and his assistant, a young Mpogoro man from nearby Morogoro, whose job was evidence of the fruits of independence for *wananchi*, since during the colonial days everything to do with accounts in white people's business firms as well as in the Civil Service was exclusively employment for whites and Indians only. The two employees had likewise stood up when their master came in. Mnyapara Munubi had been quicker and greeted their boss and told him why he wanted to see him before them. They too now came closer to their employer so as to speak to him. Before they could say a word, their boss roughly pushed them away with both his hands and went to his Camp Headman. The white man was also tall and big, but could stand no higher than Mnyapara Munubi's chin. He stood very close to him as if he wanted to bite his chin and began to holler at him, his saliva jetting out of his mouth and landing all over

Mnyapara Munubi's face, "You want make trouble for my plantation!"

"What trouble, Master? I have only come to inform you that I got married and I have moved and gone to live with my wife outside the camp, in my own house. I have come to return to you the key of the camp house I lived in."

His English employer could contain his anger no more. To him the only use that giant had was protecting his farm and keeping everything there safe. That was why he had given him the title of Camp Headman, even though his real work remained the usual one of a master's foreman, driving his fellow laborers to work hard for their master. It was because a giant like him lived in the barracks of his plantation that problems of workers drunkenness and fighting so common in the camps of other farm owners were unknown on his. No property of his on the plantation had ever been stolen, and no armed robbers had ever attempted to break into his workshop or his office. All those problems which plagued business owners since black people got their so-called *Uhuru* were completely unknown to him, because everybody knew the giant lived on his farm. And now the creature he was paying his money to work for him and do his bidding wanted to be a master too, with his own home, which mattered to him more than his property, his employer's property! The white man was so angry words stuck in his throat! And when they came out again, they came accompanied with actions: "Out of here, now! You hear! Out of here!" he shouted, a finger on one hand pointing to the door and the other hand pushing his Camp Headman. "Out of here, I say! Stupid savage!..."

Mnyapara Munubi was stupefied! He simply could not understand why his employer was angry. He wanted to explain himself, because it was possible his employer hadn't understood him. He was sure once he understood he would have no reason to be angry with him, since, even though he would be living outside the farm, he would continue to work for him as usual. But, by force of habit, all the masters' *mnyapara* of so many years did was to simply obey his employer's order. He lowered his head and turned around and made for the door as ordered, while his lord and master on his side accompanied him with more insults: "Damn you, savage! Stupid idiot! Bloody fool!..." However as he stepped out of the door and raised his head again to retrace his steps well, he found his way blocked by his friend of many years, his visitor from the land of the dead, Mzee Jabiri, accompanied by his son Saidi in their usual way. And, as usual, the old man was completely naked and still carrying his wounds of the whip and dripping with shit and blood from the grey hair on his head to the soles of his feet! Mzee Jabiri too was pointing a finger, for Mnyapara Munubi to retrace his steps and go back to the office he had just left. He accompanied his pointing finger with sharp word: "The days of a white person calling an African 'savage' are over. This is independent Tanganyika, where all people are equal. The rich and the poor are all equal fellow human beings. If you allow this colonial foreigner to treat you like his plaything, then you are indeed a savage and an idiot! You don't even deserve to be called a man, worthy of marrying a woman like Eliza!"

The two other employees who were in the office, the Indian accountant and his *Mswahili*[14] assistant, as well as all the messengers and clerks who were in the office at the time and saw what happened, when they took the witness stand in court all testified that the accused, the Camp Headman of their farm, Paulo, came out of the plantation office, where he had been quarreling with their employer, and then stood still outside the door, as if he was debating with himself whether to go or to come back. Then he turned around and came back straight to their employer, who was still standing where he left him in the office lounge, and there and then struck him with a fist in the chest and knocked him down flat on his back. He then knelt down and made a sign of the cross, like a person praying, before striking him with another fist, again in the chest. After that he stood up, went out of the office and walked away, without turning to look back, not even once. On his part, the accused too kept on saying one and the same thing from the beginning of the trial to the end: that he did what he did on the orders of Mzee Jabiri who came from the land of the dead and commanded him to do so. The judge and his assessors had therefore no doubt that the accused was pretending to be insane so as not to face the consequences of his actions. And since he wasn't denying to have done what the eye witnesses said he did and as a result caused the death of their employer, he was found guilty of premeditated murder as charged and sentenced to death by hanging, while he continued to proclaim his innocence, saying that he had simply obeyed orders, from heaven.

In explaining his judgment and the death sentence, the High Court Judge wrote that the accused, a man of such a terrifying physique, knew very well what his bodily strength was capable of. Therefore, when he knocked down the deceased with a single blow of the fist in the chest and the deceased remained flat on the ground and he still decided to strike him with another fist, again in the chest, he had intended to kill him and wanted to make sure he was dead. On their part, most of the Africans of independent Tanganyika who flocked to the High Court daily to have a glimpse of the man or who read in the newspapers the sensational murder case of Big Mmakonde who flattened the chest of a white man with a single blow of the fist for daring to call him "savage!" did not agree with that judgment. "It is only because the accused is a black man and the man who was killed was white and our judges too are still all white. Had the man who was killed been black and the accused white there wouldn't have been any case. It would have been simply 'Dismiss case' right away! Even if two black men or two white men had such a quarrel and as a result one of them died, it would still be a very different case, because the accused was provoked. Any man who calls another man 'stupid savage' and pushes him around as if he were his wife is courting trouble!" *wananchi* of Tanganyika-*huru* claimed.

The East African Court of Appeal however agreed with the white judge and Mnyapara Munubi was duly hanged. And when he was hanged in that year of 1962, at the age of forty-five, the white masters' Mnyapara Mkuu became the first *mwananchi* to be executed with a death warrant signed by President Nyerere, the first President of independent Tanganyika. And the person who took the death warrant to President Nyerere's table for the signature authorizing his execution was none other than Saidi, the son of Mzee Jabiri, Mnyapara Munubi's dear old man who came from the land of the dead to command him never again to be a white person's plaything.

PART III

Ndugu Saidi

7

Saidi himself was unaware of all that. And he was now no longer a boy but a grown man with a wife and a home of his own, already reviving his grandparents clans as his late father, Mzee Jabiri, counseled him before departing from this world. He was also *mwananchi* and *mzalendo*[15] with what was for him an important job, for he was an employee of *Ikulu*,[16] serving the President of his young nation and the Chairman of TANU, the liberation party of the people of Tanganyika, the Most Most Honorable Julius Kambarage Nyerere.

At Mr. Tumbo Tumbo's plantation Saidi was not a real farm laborer but the son of a farmworker who had been allowed to stay on the plantation because his father had nowhere to leave him. He was therefore not likely to be in trouble for running away from the farm. All the same, white employers were unpredictable, and so it was still necessary to make sure nobody knew where he was hiding. When finally arrangements were made and he traveled to Dar es Salaam, he was met in the city by Grandma Ntwara, a Mmakonde relative of Mnyapara Munubi and his fellow Mmakonde who had been hiding the boy. The woman was a nanny of very many years in India-town[17] of the city, and in no time she found the boy entrusted to her by her relatives too a job in India-town. He became a houseboy there.

Saidi's new job in India-town was washing the clothes of his employer's family, cleaning their house, helping to cook their food, washing dishes, in addition to being sent on endless errands from morning till evening with no moment of rest, so that he was a real slave of his employers. But Saidi, a boy who at the age of ten could stand the full workload of an adult sisal farm laborer, was more than equal to it. Except that one of the children of his new employer decided to make his job of a houseboy unusually trying!

The Indian couple he was working for had two children, a boy and a girl. Grandma Ntwara had in other words managed to find an easy job for his young man, because he would be working for Indian employers who didn't have a house overflowing with children. The older of the two children of Saidi's employers, the boy, was seven years old and had begun going to school, and his younger sister was four and remained at home the whole day. On the very first day Saidi started working at their parents' home, the boy called him and informed him he wanted to go to the toilet: "Saidi, I am going to shit!" shouting at the top of his voice from far away, and Saidi couldn't understand why that Indian boy wanted him to know he was going to relieve himself! And when the boy didn't see their new houseboy at once follow him into the toilet to attend to him as their other houseboys usually did, he concluded he was a stubborn one and decided to teach him a lesson. The boy, and likewise his sister, no longer wet their beds. But from that day the boy deliberately wet and shit in bed every morning before waking up. And so right from the start Saidi was forced to wash with his hands the shit and urine of that fully grown child of his employers as part of his job of a houseboy. Daily! And nobody knows for how long his ordeal would have lasted had the boy's sister not come to his rescue.

His employers' clothe-shop was on the ground floor of a building on Morogoro Road, and the owners lived upstairs in the same building, directly above their shop, in an apartment where each of their two children had a room of his own and her own. The parents were the first to wake up, very early in the morning, to get the shop ready for business. Then the boy of despicable doings woke up, to go to school. Then finally, and very much later, the young girl of four years woke up too, to go and join the crowd of children of the other Indian shop owners who lived in other apartments on the upper levels of the big building. The very first thing Saidi did every morning when he arrived at work was to clean the house and to change bedsheets and make the beds. So every morning Saidi started off his work by hauling a load of the shit and urine of that grown up Indian brat to the washing room and forcing himself to wash it! Because his employer and his wife at that time would have already gone downstairs to the shop and their daughter would still be asleep, their son's filthy doings remained a secret known only to Saidi and the boy himself. And that went on for three and a half months.

One morning when Saidi arrived at work his employer sent him on an errand to Upanga, to the home of a fellow Indian businessman, his brother-in-law, the elder brother of his wife, and didn't come back until it was time for his employer's daughter too to wake up. On waking up and finding herself all alone at home, the little girl decided to go on an inspection tour of the whole house, but especially the areas which were supposed to be out-of-bounds to her. She fist went to her parents' bedroom and inspected this and that in the room for a little while. Then she made her way to her brother's bedroom, to find out what was new in there that she wasn't supposed to touch so that she could touch and play with it as much as she wanted. As soon as she stepped into the room she was overwhelmed by the stench of her brother's misbehavior.

"Eh! What smells like shit here!" And she didn't have to look far. Her brother, in order to really teach a lesson their insolent houseboy, before getting up he would empty his bladder of its whole-night load of urine in the middle of his bed and squeeze his stomach and push really hard and heap all the shit he could get out in the middle of his urine and leave that abominable filth of his completely uncovered, so

42

that their arrogant houseboy would get a fitting welcome when he entered the room in the morning. On his sister seeing with her own eyes his brother's misdeeds, she said to herself she had finally got that brother of his, who, simply because he went to school and was older, thought he knew everything and considered her a worthless being! And so, shouting and yelling and spitting without pause, she left the room and ran downstairs to their parents in the shop, on her way startling a crowd of other Indian children and their mothers and nannies and houseboys all over the apartments upstairs. It was now ten o'clock in the morning and her parents' shop was already open and customers were beginning to stream in. The young girl decided that the best way of really teaching a lesson his brother, their parents' favorite who they adored so much, was to let each and everybody in the shop know what a most disgusting creature he was. So she shouted at the top of her voice in all the languages she knew, Hindi, Indian Swahili, Swahili-Hindi, Indian-English that her elder brother was still wetting and shitting in his bed. By the time her mother got into the room of her first born, their house was overflowing with onlookers, all shaking their heads at the strange doings of her son. That was how that Indian young girl saved Saidi from the bane of his new job the son of his employers was deliberately subjecting him to. The Indian boy's ugly mischief, instead of punishing their new houseboy for his arrogance, made the boy himself a laughingstock to his friends and shamed his parents. And also put an end to his sinister pranks.

Saidi was such a hardworking boy that his employer as well his wife liked him right from his first day at work. They were ashamed of the disgusting things their son had made their diligent and very likable employee endure and, because they did not want to lose him, decided to move him to the shop as a helping hand. And from that day Saidi was saved from the shit and urine of the children of his Indian masters and became their shop employee.

Saidi worked in his Indian employers' shop sweeping, cleaning windows, dusting merchandise, welcoming customers, being sent on errands to the post office, the bank, and here and there and everywhere from the time the shop opened in the morning until it closed in the evening for a period of nine years.

8

*O*n the seventh of July, 1954, Julius Kambarage Nyerere, a teacher at Pugu Secondary School, in Mwakanga village, Kisarawe District, on the outskirts of the city of Dar es Salaam, together with eleven fellow *wananchi* from different parts of Tanganyika, founded TANU, Tanganyika African National Union, a political party for the liberation of the African in the country. And *wananchi* of the city of Dar es Salaam welcomed with their heart and soul the politics of the new party. People in the city and all over the country talked of nothing else but TANU and its politics of their liberation.

When Saidi arrived in the city he stayed with Grandma Ntwara, the elderly Mmakonde woman who had received him. The name Ntwara was a nickname people had given her because of the way she pronounced Mtwara, her place of origin of which she never tired of talking and praising. She lived on Twiga Street in Kariakoo, next door to the *Uswahilini*[18] house in which TANU was born and which became the party's headquarters. Saidi was such a well behaved boy that the Mmakonde woman right away loved him like a son, and he continued to stay at her home for several years. And when he finally rented a place of his own, it was a room Grandma Ntwara had found him very close to her place in Kariakoo, so that she could always check on him to see how life in the city was treating her young man. Saidi was therefore living next door to TANU headquarters, and when the party for the liberation of the Africans from white people's colonialism and oppression launched its TANU Youth League, he, who knew all about colonial oppression, was among the very first youths in the country to join the party's youth wing.

In those early days TANU had virtually no money at all, so that almost every work at the party headquarters depended on volunteers. And TANU Party headquarters became the place where you found Saidi on Saturday afternoons, after his toil in India-town ended, as well as on weekdays in the evening after the Indians shop owners closed their businesses for the day. In the end, Nyerere took him for a son of one of the Party Elders, Mzee Rupia and his fellow elders, brought there to help with work. Consequently one Thursday in 1956, at about two in the afternoon, Nyerere told one of the officers at the party headquarters to call Saidi for him at once.

"Saidi at this time is still at his place of work," Nyerere's office assistant told him.

"I see! All the time I took him for one of our own young men here, so he works somewhere else!"

"He comes to volunteer for work, Your Honor, otherwise he works in the city center. In the shops of the Indians, I understand."

"If that is the case, his place is here. We need a permanent help in the office, and this young man would be great for us. As a matter of fact I assumed he was a Msukuma young man, brought here by our elder, Mzee Rupia, to help us with work!" Mzee Rupia was at the party headquarters that afternoon and the President of TANU Party turned to look at him while saying that. Mzee Rupia answered him, equally truthfully, that he too took Saidi for a Mzanaki young man, the son of the relatives of the president of their party, and everybody in the office laughed. And from that day Saidi stopped being a shop-boy of an Indian businessman and became an employee of the party fighting for the independence of *wananchi* of Tanganyika.

Saidi's employment at TANU headquarters was also work without rest from morning till evening, hardly any better than his job at the

Indian's shop. In fact it was work at all hours of the day, with no time for rest, at night or during daytime, Saturdays, Sundays and holidays alike. At any time the leaders of the party for the liberation of *wananchi* could be having a meeting at the office, talking with some *wananchi*, receiving a foreign delegation, confronting this or that provocation by the colonial government. Saidi could therefore be required to be at the office any time during daytime or at night. Officially he was employed as a messenger, but, since he was the only helping hand at the office, his work included sweeping and mopping the floor of all the offices in the building and attending to whatever work there was to do at the office and for party officials, including their personal errands. And his wages, due to the miserable financial condition of the party at the time, were even less than the meager pay he used to get at the Indian's shop. And he had been warned from the beginning that, because of the party's lack of revenue, he should be prepared in some months to be paid late and in others not to be paid at all until the situation improved. But Saidi accepted all that very gladly and with real gratitude for being given the opportunity to serve TANU, the party fighting for the rights of black people and all the weak of the country, because he, Saidi, knew perhaps more than anybody else in the world what the inhumanity and contempt of white people for the Africans meant, and what it meant to be a weak person who can be oppressed and humiliated by a master with impunity.

And so Saidi, in spite of the difficult demands of his work, dedicated himself entirely to his new job at the TANU headquarters his heart overflowing with a boundless sense of patriotism. Finally, on December 9, 1961, Tanganyika gained its *Uhuru*.

When Tanganyika became independent, Honorable Nyerere, the President of TANU, became the Prime Minister of the Government of his country but at the same time remained president of the party, dividing his time between the Prime Minister's Office and TANU

Party Headquarters, where Saidi continued to work for him and for their party. Then when in 1962 Tanganyika became a republic and Nyerere his country's Head of State and he moved to *Ikulu* as the first President of independent Tanganyika, he wanted brought to him his messenger from the party headquarters, a young man who had worked for him for many years, a dedicated worker, a person of unimpeachable character and an exemplary *mzalendo*. So Saidi went to *Ikulu* of his country to work for President Nyerere, having been chosen for the job by the Father of his Nation himself on account of his hard work and his patriotism.

9

Saidi was now no longer a boy but a young man of more than twenty years of age. And God had been kind to him and he had a job in the President's Office. He therefore felt the time had come for him to fulfill his late father's wish: marry and try to revive their clan.

All those years in the city, the only thing Saidi cared for was his work. From the time he was a houseboy in India-town through adolescence and until he reached that age when a man desires to have a wife in his life, to him having a good time and the pleasures of the city were things he only heard people talk about. Women too, however beautiful, did not concern him, with the result that his friends doubted whether he was a real man, because they had never seen him with a woman. And so when he felt he should get married he had no fiancée or a young woman he knew well enough to want to be engaged to. And so he made a trip in search of his adoptive mother in the city, Grandma Ntwara, to talk to her about it and see whether she could help him.

Grandma Ntwara was no longer a nanny of the Indians. On the eve of independence Grandma Ntwara had told her fellow nannies and the houseboys of India-town that when independence came she would no longer live by fondling the urine and shit of other people's children. Her fellow employees took that to be nothing but another of Grandma Ntwara's banter, because all around their place of work there was no one better at cracking jokes and spinning tales than that woman with her Kimakonde-Swahili. But that was what happened. Grandma

Ntwara celebrated the independence of their country by saying goodbye to her job of very many years in India-town of the city of Dar es Salaam! And that was not all. The woman who used to make them laugh so much was among the very first *wananchi* to live in their own houses, brand new and fully paid for, built with the assistance of self-help projects in several low-income districts of the city. Grandma Ntwara's house was among those built in Magomeni. It was a six-room house, with outer bathroom and kitchen and a small house behind the main house, and all the buildings fenced in by a concrete-brick wall. Her former domestic workers of India-town were left shaking their heads and having to admit that Grandma Ntwara was indeed something else!

Grandma Ntwara had a grown up daughter in her native Mtwara, and when she moved into her house in Magomeni her daughter came to Dar es Salaam to live with her. She was a divorced woman with two children, a boy of seven and his younger sister three years of age. And so now Grandma Ntwara was someone living in her own home with her daughter and grandchildren, and no longer an Indian's nanny renting tiny rooms at the back of the compound of a house in overcrowded Kariakoo streets where she lived for ages. And the new job of Grandma Ntwara by which she made her living in Tanganyika-*huru* was cooking and selling food. As soon as she moved into her house and her daughter came to live with her, she began cooking rice with beans for selling to the inhabitants of the surrounding streets, especially young men and bachelors who found cooking a bother. Her food was well prepared and deliciously seasoned with coconut milk, and she served it generously and at a very reasonable price compared with the price of plain or biryan rice in the restaurants of the Arabs. As a consequence she had plenty of customers right away. That was Grandma Ntwara's way of answering TANU Party's call of *Uhuru* with Work and Self-reliance. In addition to that, she had renters in three of the six main house rooms and in the two rooms of the small house at the back of her compound. That was the changed life of Grandma Ntwara in independent Tanganyika.

Saidi went to see that mother of his on a Saturday morning. He found her and her daughter and grandchildren all busy picking debris from rice and grating coconuts for making coconut milk in preparation for their food business in the evening. Saidi joined them and spent the whole day helping them with their work. And when in the evening he caught a bus to take him back to his room in Kariakoo, he could hardly contain his happiness. His mother, Grandma Ntwara, had been delighted with his decision to get married and had promised to help him find a fiancée.

And indeed in no time Grandma Ntwara had looked for and found a fiancée for his young man, and that same year, 1962, Saidi was married. The couple was married in Magomeni Mosque, and his new bride was Chiku daughter of Bakari, a young woman of eighteen years of age, the daughter of Grandma Ntwara's relatives who lived in nearby Kinondoni, a girl Grandma Ntwara had known since she was born. Their wedding celebrations were held at Grandma Ntwara's Magomeni home, and what a great occasion it was! And Saidi started his life of an adult man with a household to look after.

10

*1*967 was the year of the proclamation of the Arusha Declaration, a great event in the history of Tanganyika, now called Mainland-Tanzania, after the country united with Zanzibar in 1964 to form the United Republic of Tanzania. The main objective of the Arusha Declaration was to end the exploitation of the people and quickly bring equality and prosperity for all *wananchi*. And among the steps taken to realize the objective of the country's *Ujamaa*[19] policy of ending once and for all the exploitation of the people was the nationalization of all big private businesses and capitalist enterprises in the country and the establishing of public corporations to take over those pillars of the nation's economy and make them the property of the people and run them for the benefit and welfare of *wananchi*. The most important of the public corporations created was the Projects, Wealth, Savings and National Development Corporation. The person Mwalimu[20] Nyerere appointed to run that important public corporation was Ndugu Nzoka, a great friend of Saidi. Like Saidi, Nzoka too was a young TANU man of since the days of the struggle for independence. He too was working at the party headquarters until the independence of their country, and was moved from there to *Ikulu* by Mwalimu at the same time in 1962 the President decided to bring Saidi to work for him in *Ikulu*. When both were working at the party headquarters, where Saidi was a messenger, his fellow TANU young man, Nzoka, was one of the party assistant secretaries helping Nyerere with the propagation of the party in the country. And when Mwalimu Nyerere became President of the Republic of Tanzania and wanted his two trusted and politically mature young men to help him with work in *Ikulu*, Nzoka became the President's Special Assistant for Internal Affairs and Politics. And when that all important public corporation was created in the Arusha Declaration year, Ndugu Nzoka, a young man of about thirty yeas of age, the age of his friend Saidi, was entrusted with the responsibility of running the corporation as its Executive Chairman. When he found himself promoted to such a high ranking post, he too decided to lift up his friend Saidi and asked President Nyerere to allow him to make Saidi the Head Messenger of his new corporation. The Head Messenger of *Ikulu* was the one inherited from the colonial regime, since Mwalimu Nyerere had no reason for taking away that *mwananchi's* job or lowering his rank. The President of Tanzania had therefore no objection, and was indeed delighted to see his new Executive Chairman of a public corporation wanting to reward due merit in a fellow party faithful.

The position of Head Messenger of the new public corporation made Saidi feel really blessed. To begin with, his salary was twice what he was getting in *Ikulu*. These new public corporations had inherited capitalist and multinational businesses whose employees had fat salaries and attractive fringe benefits, which they continued to receive, since it would have been inexplicable to reduce the salaries *wananchi* had been getting or to give the new employees of the corporations anything less. Also being head is being head, even as a messenger. So Saidi too, for the first time in his life, became an employee who could take a bit of rest at work and who had subordinates he too could send on errands.

At home too God had answered his late father's prayer and his wife Chiku gave birth to children soon after they were married. First she gave birth to a boy, in 1963, to whom Saidi gave the name of his dear departed father, Jabiri. When Grandma Ntwara came to see them after the birth of their son to congratulate them and bring them presents for the child, she also advised them regarding that blessing of the Almighty God, having children, by telling them how important it was for a husband to allow his wife time to rest after giving birth and not to resume making love to her until the nursing child had been weaned. And Saidi and Chiku did so. When their son Jabiri was weaned, after he had suckled for a whole year, God continued to bless them and they got another child in 1965, this time a baby girl. Saidi named her Idaya, the name of his dear late mother. And in the year of the Arusha Declaration, Chiku gave birth to yet another child, this time too a baby girl, whom Saidi named after his departed beloved sister Amina.

Saidi's wife Chiku was the first born of her parents and had many younger brothers and sisters. Long before they had their first child, soon after they got married, the couple had gone together to Chiku's parents to ask for a child to stay with and bring up. "A child to send for a cup of water to drink and to cheer up our home so that it doesn't feel like the inside of a bush or an anthill, where no sound of a child is ever heard." Chiku's parents gave them Tabu, a younger sister of hers who was in the third grade of primary school. And when Chiku gave birth to her first child the couple went back to her parents to look for a young girl to help her take care of her newborn. Her parents got for them a young girl of twelve, a daughter of relatives of theirs who was not attending school. And when Chiku gave birth to more children, that daughter of her relatives stayed on and lived with them.

So in that year of the Arusha Declaration when Chiku gave birth to her third child Ndugu Saidi's household in his Kariakoo home already comprised seven people, who lived in two rooms of a *Uswahilini* house into which Saidi moved as he was about to get married, after living for many years in a nearby tiny room at the back of a house-compound he rented when he left Grandma Ntwara's, his first home on arriving in the city.

One Saturday morning in that same year of 1967 Saidi paid another special visit to his mother, Grandma Ntwara, at her Magomeni home.

Grandma Ntwara of Magomeni was now a very well established businesswoman. Her freelance business of selling rice with beans in an unlicensed restaurant had greatly expanded. She no longer rented the two rooms of the small house at the back of her compound, and instead she had turned them into a full-fledged restaurant which served food night and day. And now she was not selling only rice and beans. One could now eat everything there, especially food people liked but which was never sold at the restaurants of the Arabs: rice with spinach, *ugali*[21] with meat, *ugali* with fish, *ugali* with spinach, plantain with meat, cow-hoof soup and stewed goat-head meat, and at really affordable prices. As a result customers were all the time flocking into her restaurant and she had had to hire some help, two women from her ethnic group. In addition to her restaurant business, she had erected a small *genge*[22] adjacent to her house, where she stocked commodities in great household demand like coconuts, tomatoes, onions, salt, spinach, oranges and mangoes, for selling to the residents of her neighborhood to save them the trouble of going all the way to Magomeni Market every time they needed such small things. At her *genge* is where now you found Grandma Ntwara with her endless tales and jokes in her comic Swahili. Her daughter was now the one in charge of the restaurant business. In addition, her daughter had also started another freelance business in their house, which was also bringing them a lot of money. She had opened a beer store. The main house too had no single renter remaining. Of the three rooms on the side of the house which had renters, now one was for storing crates of beer and soda and the remaining two were a place where people in search of a good time who disliked the noise and commotion of bars came to enjoy their cold bear in private and at lower prices than in those noisy bars with their rowdy riffraff fighting over barmaids. Both rooms now had a huge refrigerator each and were furnished with beautiful couches. And the beer store of the daughter of Grandma Ntwara of Magomeni had already become the preferred rendezvous of big shots from all over the city. People had decided to nickname Grandma Ntwara's daughter Mama Ntwara as soon she arrived in the city, and her beer store was also popularly known as "At Mama Ntwara's". And the real reason behind its fame was that daughter of Grandma Ntwara herself. God of that Mmakonde woman of about thirty-five years of age so created her that any man who laid eyes on her and looked at her really well and saw her body and the way she moved was bound to dream of her at night! And that was the woman who was serving at her Magomeni beer store *wananchi vizito*[23] of Dar es Salaam who wanted to have a good time in private!

This time, Saidi went to Magomeni to seek Grandma Ntwara's advice on his intention to build a house. The two rooms he rented could no longer do for his growing family. Even if they could still do, when God has willed to bless a man with children he has a duty to build them a house if he can, so that his children have a place they call home, since a rented house never belongs to the renter.

This time again Grandma Ntwara was really pleased with what Saidi went to tell her: "My son, you have now become an adult! You were married and with children, yes, but you hadn't grown up! But now that you have decided to build for your wife and your children a home of their own, you are a grown-up!" she congratulated his young man.

From the very first day he started working in the city, Saidi did his best to save a bit from the little he was paid. That was the advice her adoptive mother in the city, Grandma Ntwara, gave him when she found him his first job as an Indian family's houseboy. That too was what he always felt he had to do, because that was what work meant to him from the time he was a little boy cutting sisal with adult laborers in Tanga where his late father, Mzee Jabiri, died. He had therefore saved quite a bit, given his modest income. To prepare himself well for his undertaking, he had taken out a loan of 10,000 shillings from his corporation to add to his savings. Among the fringe benefits for the employees of their new corporation was a loan of up to 20,000 shillings each from the corporation for building a house for low salary workers, who did not qualify for house construction loans from the National Housing Bank. Saidi had estimated that he would need only half of the maximum loan amount, given his savings, and because he did not want to burden himself with too big a debt unnecessarily.

"Because you have decided to make the bricks yourself during your annual leave, you have enough money for the job," Gradma Ntwara encouraged him, genuinely happy to see how well he had prepared himself for his important task.

The following week Grandma Ntwara had already looked for and found a plot of land for him, in Manzese, where a person got a plot at once from the owners of the land without having to wait for ever for a surveyed plot from the city land officers. She and her daughter had already built two houses in Manzese, which they were renting to tenants. And, without loss of time, Saidi took his annual leave and began making concrete bricks for the construction of a home for his family.

Unfortunately things didn't go as Saidi and Grandma Ntwara had expected. Saidi had finished making the bricks and procuring all the other necessary materials and the construction of the house had begun when bad luck befell his family. His elder daughter, Idaya, now about three years of age, caught a disease for which they couldn't find a cure. It began as a fever, which turned into *degedege*[24] which almost took her away from this world. Fortunately Grandma Ntwara warned Saidi and Chiku in time that *degedege* did not take well to European medicine, especially injections, and they looked for a traditional healer who cured their child of the dangerous children's disease. But even after she was cured of *degedege* the child did not get well. Now every time she ate anything immediately she threw up. Saidi and Chiku took their child back to the hospital, but all in vain. They took her again to traditional healers of every kind, again to no avail. In the end the child became nothing but bare bones and a skull out of which her eyes protruded! At the same time she was crying day and night, without ever letting down. Even mere neighbors could hardly contain their tears when they looked at her! And yet her mother was nursing another baby! Chiku had no choice but to wean her baby prematurely so as to devote all her time to finding a cure for their sick child. To make matters worse, she no longer had someone to help her take care of her children. Her young cousin who had been living with her since she gave birth to her first child had gone back to her parents that same year because she had reached puberty and her parents wanted to begin looking for a husband for her. Fortunately she still lived with her younger sister Tabu, who did not continue with school when she finished eighth grade. Chiku's younger sister now became the second mother of her newly weaned baby while she herself did all she could to find a healer for her sick child, all alone, since Saidi had to continue working to support their family. For months on end she traveled all over the country looking for a cure for her child, but again to no avail! Finally God took pity of the couple. Their child at long last responded well to the medicine of a Msukuma healer somewhere in far off Geita where Chiku had ended up with the child. The child began eating food normally again. Slowly she got stronger and regained her body and became a healthy child once more. Only then did Saidi resume the construction of his house in Manzese, after nearly two years had gone by, and after the greater part of his savings intended for the construction of the house had been spent on looking for a cure for their sick child.

As a result, Saidi did not move into his house in Manzese in 1968 as he had intended but in 1970, and he moved in before the house was completed.

Saidi's home in Manzese was a *banda*[25] with fours bedrooms and a sitting room. Grandma Ntwara had advised him to build behind the main house a small house with three rooms for renting, but, because of the sickness of their child and the money they spent on finding her a cure, that had not been possible. The only thing he had managed to build at the back of his compound was a hut of wood-and-wattle plastered with clay mud for use as a kitchen until his money situation improved a bit. A hut of wood-and-wattle was also all he could afford for a latrine. He had also run short of cement and, when he moved in, he had managed to plaster with mortar only the outside of the main house, and the floor of the house too was of beaten earth. Plastering the inside of the house with mortar and a cement floor for the house had also to wait. Putting a ceiling over the rooms too had to wait. He had likewise run short of money for timber for making door-shutters. Fortunately a few corrugated iron sheets remained after roofing the house, and he used them to make shutters for the doors and windows of the house. Saidi had been determined that his house, whatever else it may lack, must have electric lights, but there too he had to make do with tin-can paraffin lamps, until later. He had likewise to wait until later before he could have running tap water in his house. All the same, Saidi and his wife and their children moved into their house and lived in a home of their own.

Because of the sickness of their daughter Idaya, Saidi and Chiku delayed longer than usual before trying to get another child after the birth of Amina, their third child. But when their child recovered fully they resumed their normal life of husband and wife and God continued to bless them. When they moved into their new house in June of that year of 1970 Chiku was already pregnant again for three months, and in December that year the Almighty God blessed their new home by giving them a forth child, another baby girl. Saidi and Chiku decided to name the child Bibi[26] Ntwara, Bibi for short. Their beloved Mmakonde mother, the only friend and relative Saidi had in the world, had died about two months before from diabetes, after staying in Muhimbili Hospital for a whole month. Giving her name to their daughter was their way of thanking the departed woman for having been so good to both of them. The Almighty God continued to shower the couple with graces and in 1972 Chiku gave birth to their fifth child, this time a boy. Saidi named the child Sefu, after the newborn's grandfather, Mwene Sefu, the father of Saidi's late mother Idaya. And two years later Chiku had another child, this time a girl. Saidi named the child Mariamu, his mother-in-law, the mother of his wife Chiku. After suckling Mariamu for a whole year and weaning the child, this time Chiku stayed for two years without becoming pregnant again, so that inwardly Saidi as well as Chiku herself were convinced that most likely that was the end of the blessings God had allotted them, that Chiku had no more children in her womb. They were however still God's favorites and, at the beginning of 1977, Chiku became pregnant again and gave birth to a baby boy before the end of the year. Saidi named the child Bakari, his father-in-law, the father of the mother of his children, the grandfather of their children. Because of that, the child grew up being called Babu.[27] And two years after that Chiku gave birth to another male child. This time Saidi decided to have a namesake and named the child Saidi. The newborn therefore became Saidi. The child's mother as well as their neighbors preferred to call the child Mzee, short for Mzee Saidi. The newborn's elder brother, Babu, now two years old and still learning how to speak, turned Mzee into Majee, and everybody at home, children and adults alike, preferred that Majee to Mzee and the child grew up with Majee as his name. God continued to bless the couple and in 1981 Chiku gave birth to another child, a baby girl. Saidi decided it was time to honor the mother herself, his dear wife, and called their ninth child Chiku. To differentiate her from her mother, everybody called the newborn child Chiku-*Mdogo*.[28] The neighbors decided to embellish the child's name a bit and called her Chiku-Dogodogo. And the ninth child of Saidi and Chiku grew up being called simply Dogodogo.

What more can God grant a human being on this earth!

11

*I*n 1981, the year Dogodogo was born, Tanzania had become a very different country from the Tanzania of 1967, the year of the proclamation of the Arusha Declaration, especially for the ordinary *wananchi* like Saidi. It was true the objective of the Arusha Declaration of developing *ujamaa* and equality had succeeded in making all Tanzanians, big and small, old and young, manager and messenger, feel equal as human beings and address each other as *Ndugu*, throughout the country. The Cabinet Minister was Ndugu Minister, and he addressed a messenger like Saidi as Ndugu Messenger Saidi. Even the President of the country was Ndugu *Rais*. The truth however was that in real life equality began and ended with that term of address, *Ndugu*. And regarding *ujamaa* prosperity for all, Saidi and ordinary people like him all over the country no longer knew what to believe and not to believe! The only thing they knew for certain was that all of a sudden everything had gone so wrong that ordinary *wananchi* like Saidi could no longer make ends meet. Exactly when did things begin to go wrong and why, nobody seemed to know. And each time the Government took steps to remedy the situation things simply got worse. Whenever Saidi tried to remember when exactly things began to unravel to that extent in the country, he found he couldn't even remember what went wrong first and what followed! He was simply confronted by an impossible situation everywhere!

Saidi did not even remember he ever had the intention of completing the construction of his house when they moved in. All

Saidi and his wife Chiku thought about now, day and night, was what to do so that their children would not starve to death and can continue with their schooling. All the same, they tried their best to make their *banda* in Manzese livable for their children and the home of a happy and loving family. Chiku swept it clean, boiled water for pouring on their wooden beds and sunned the children's beddings daily without fail. She also kept a cat. So even though her home was full of children and her house had walls of bare bricks and beaten earth for a floor, Chiku's children never knew how a bedbug, tick or lice looked like, and no rat dared step into her house, when all over their neighborhood in Manzese people could hardly sleep at night from rats gnawing at their feet and lice and bedbugs feasting on their blood.

In addition to their nine children, Saidi and Chiku were also raising in their Manzese home the children of Tabu, Chiku's younger sister they took from her parents when she was still a little girl soon after they got married and raised her until she was an adult. She was now a grown-up woman who had married and divorced and then remarried. She was married the first time in 1969, and right away gave birth to children in a manner Grandma Ntwara advised Saidi and Chiku to avoid when God blessed them with their first child. She had her first child in February 1971, then in January 1972 she had the second one, and in December that same year she gave birth to her third child. She gave birth to her third child while at her sister Chiku's home in Manzese and did not go back to her husband. Her suffering at the hands of her husband had started almost from the day they were married, and even though Tabu did everything possible to make their marriage work she finally couldn't take it anymore, in spite of the fact that they were already blessed with children. Her husband was an accountant at the University of Dar es Salaam, a young Mjita man from Musoma. But, in spite of his good job, he was a disgusting drunkard who did not know or care how his wife and children lived or what they ate! And whenever he returned home full of booze, it did not matter whether his wife had just given birth or was nine months pregnant, he would slap and kick her and for no reason at all! Such animal behavior was what to him was being a real man, a "tough guy", "formidable rock", "true master of his wife!" Saidi and Chiku as well as Tabu's parents agreed with her that he was no husband but a senseless brute. She had run to her sister's place in Manzese after her labor had begun and gave birth shortly after, while those present held their breath not knowing whether the mother and her child would live or not, because her husband had beaten her so severely in spite of her being in labor! After that, Tabu's relatives went to her husband and forced him to give their daughter a divorce. Tabu with her three children then lived with Chiku, her elder sister who had brought her up. Finally she got married again, in 1974. And, thank God, this time she got married to a gentle man, even if he didn't have a big job. He was a young messenger working in Saidi's corporation, who used to come often to visit his old man from work. That was how he knew Tabu and they became friends and their friendship led to love and marriage. But, even after she remarried, the children of her first marriage continued to live with their senior mother[29] and her husband Saidi at their Manzese home. Saidi and Chiku did not deem it right to burden Tabu's second husband with bringing up the children of her first marriage, when they who brought her up from the time she was a little girl could help, especially since when she remarried she was blessed again with more children and by 1981 had given birth to three more.

Saidi and his wife Chiku in their unfinished Manzese *banda* he had once promised himself to complete were therefore struggling to bring up, feed, cloth and send to school a total of twelve children, nine their own and three their sister Tabu's, at a time when life had become simply impossible in the country.

Since he got married and was blessed with children, Saidi lived for only one thing: to give his wife and children everything they needed so that they did not know want and were happy. Not even once in his life did he think of alcohol, cigarettes, women, or any other kind of pleasure. His only happiness and pleasure was providing for his wife and children. And in past years, when life in the country still made sense and a serious minded person could plan for life and get somewhere, however modest his or her means, indeed at Saidi's home his wife and children never lacked anything they needed. But all of a sudden Saidi had seen his greatest pleasure in life of providing for his family turn into a mere dream. He could no longer even give his family the most basic food a human being needs in order to live. And he wasn't alone in that. Even people with better jobs and small families could no longer provide their households with the bare necessities of life. By that year of 1981, there was no longer any kind of fish, meat or greens minimum-wage employees, or even medium income people, could buy on their salaries alone in order to feed their families! Fish and meat had become food for the wealthy only, nobody knew since when. Even *kauzu*,[30] the tiny dry sardines from Kigoma which used to save a poor person in times of need had become impossible to buy!

Even beans had become impossible to find, and where they were found they were sold at *"kuruka"*[31] prices! And as to rice, it was no use even mentioning it. When it was found even many of those with big jobs couldn't afford it! Saidi, as a self-respecting head of a household and a man who really loved and cared for his family, had sworn he was ready to deprive himself of everything to make sure his children would never hang at the doors of other people's houses and invite themselves to food in the homes of neighbors where they smelt good food cooking and frying. Now he faced the reality that his children knew even the most ordinary food by smell only! Rice with meat, even rice with beans, to his children had become food they could only smell in the homes of the lucky ones! Even *yanga*[32] flour was something the likes of Saidi could hardly afford! Even salt! As to sugar, that was simply out of the question! Tea with loaves of bread, which in the past used to be the daytime food for the children of ordinary people, had also become something only the wealthy could afford, since wheat flour had become even scarcer than the other food items. Without wheat flour, rice or cooking oil, rice-bread and wheat and rice buns, which, like bread, used to be the daytime food for children in ordinary city-street households, also disappeared from sight, and where they were found, they were sold at impossible prices!

That was the kind of life confronting the messenger Saidi son of Jabiri with his large family at his Manzese home.

Fortunately in all those difficulties Saidi's life was made a bit easier by his workplace shop. Since quite some time back the Government had opened *kaya*[33] shops in residential districts of Dar es Salaam in order to ease the shortage of food and other consumer goods for *wananchi* by ensuring that whatever little was available was distributed fairly to all the household shops and sold to people according to the size of their families and at legitimate prices. The problem with the government program was that often there wasn't anything at all for distributing to the household shops! It was therefore very usual for people to spend the whole day lining at the doors of their household shops, having been promised corn flour, or salt, or beans, and then to walk back home with their bowls and aluminum pots and baskets of all sizes and shapes still empty. And in times of such acute shortages of food and other consumer goods there was bound to be unscrupulous and greedy individuals among those entrusted with getting to *wananchi* the scarce commodities, and instead of the goods being sent to the household shops for the people, they were grabbed by those public servants and *leaders*[34] and ended

66

up on the black market, where they were sold at *kuruka* prices ordinary people like Saidi could not afford. The *kaya* shop in Saidi's neighborhood in Manzese, like the other household shops in the city, was therefore not very reliable. What Saidi relied on more was the shop in his place of work. Besides the household shops in residential districts, the Government had also set up workplace shops so as to minimize the time office and factory workers spent away from work looking for food and other essentials in the city. And big public corporations like Ndugu Saidi's always got their full allocations of everything, because their managers had access and were listened to by their colleagues in the Distribution Corporation, the National Milling Corporation, and the Regional Trading Corporation, the public corporations in charge of virtually all the food and other consumer goods in the city. In that respect, Saidi was considered lucky by his neighbors in Manzese who had nowhere else to turn to other than their household shop.

All the same, even with what he managed to get from his workplace shop, Saidi still could not feed and take care of his family properly. All the children in his home, with the exception of the very little ones, instead of breakfasting on tea with bread, rice-buns or wheat-buns as they used to do, now breakfasted on *yanga* flour porridge to which salt, in stead of sugar, had been added. And at lunch time and likewise for dinner at night they had *ugali* of the same *yanga* with beans cooked with nothing but water and salt! And on days when there were no beans the children had to force themselves to eat *yanga ugali* with ground rock salt for relish! On such days Saidi could not sleep, he wept like a child all night long, with his wife beseeching him not to give up that way! "Our children are all in good health, are growing up well behaved, and are continuing with their schooling just fine. He who gave us our children will also enable us to raise them into adults who will succeed in their lives." Saidi would answer with

"Amen!" to his wife's prayer.

But Chiku did not just console her husband with words and prayers. She did everything she could to relieve a bit the bitter existence of her family. Every time her husband managed to bring a bit of wheat flour from his workplace, she would take the last few coins she had and run to the market to buy two bottles of coconut milk oil, then come home and boil the oil to remove the stench of rotten coconut and get cooking oil good enough for making wheat-buns. Of the buns, only the very young children of her home would be given one each, to taste, and she would sell the rest at the front of her house door to passers-by, who fought over them and snatched them all off in no time since, with the scarcity of wheat and cooking oil, buns had become a rare delicacy. With the money from selling her buns she would run to the market again, to try and beat the long line of those looking for cow entrails or the paltry dry fish from Nyumba-ya-Mungu dam, to which she would add one coconut, and two tomatoes, and return home to make relish. And that day her children would eat ugali of *yanga* which at least tasted like food. On the day her husband brought cooking oil from his workplace, she would go to the market and buy cassava and fry it and sell fried cassava at the door of her house and get some money and run to the market again and once more improvise something in her kitchen. And that day too her children would eat palatable food. And the days went by and her children continued to grow.

12

*L*ife had become so difficult that for many years now Ndugu Saidi had not had any kind of festivity in his home. He could not even remember the last time he bought his children new clothes for an occasion. In the past each year on *Id el fitr*[35] every child was dressed up in beautiful new clothes and, after feasting on pilaf and plain and biryan rice and drinking soda and being treated to all kinds of delicacies, all of them were given a bit of money early in the afternoon to catch a bus to their grandma and grandpa in Kinondoni for their Idd Mbarak presents, from where they caught another bus to Mnazi Mmoja grounds in the city center to watch the games and entertainments of the holiday. That now was like something which never happened at all! Saidi could not also remember the year he bought his wife new *kanga*[36] or *vitenge*[37] the last time, and yet he never waited for a holiday or an occasion to buy her new shoes or a new pair of *kanga* or *vitenge*, so that there was a time when Chiku had several suitcases full of clothes and shoes and had even to look for relatives and friends to give some to! At that time Saidi would have considered it a great insult had someone dared to tell him to buy old clothes for his wife, clothes which had been worn by other women, but now he couldn't even afford to buy those *mitumba*,[38] ever since those rags and tatters discarded by the dead and lepers, of nobody knows which foreign shores, became the only articles of wear the have-nots of the country like him could afford! He could hardly afford to buy enough *kandambili*[39] flipflops for everybody in his home. For him personally *katambuga*[40] from old car-tires had become his only footwear since he didn't know how many years. And what saved him from walking with bare buttocks and shoulders were his work clothes. His heavy cotton messenger's jacket and pants had become his wear for all occasions, at work, at home, at funerals, at celebrations, however big, as well as at Friday prayer in the mosque.

That was the life of Saidi son of Jabiri and his family.

However, in spite of all his difficulties, Saidi had never failed to commemorate the birth of a single one of his children. Their ninth child who was born that year of 1981, Dogodogo, was born just before *Id el fitr* holiday, and Saidi decided to celebrate the birth of their child on Idi holiday, so that his children too that year would feel they had enjoyed themselves, be it only a little, on the great holiday of all Moslems. So Saidi and Chiku got busy preparing for a feast and told their dear friends and relatives to come and visit them on that day and share in their happiness. In the past, when their first child, Jabiri, and their other older children were born, the couple got ready to celebrate the birth of their child by slaughtering a goat and buying every kind of food and condiment and then prepared a real feast! The days of slaughtering a goat for a feast in Tanzania had now become a mere dream for the likes of Saidi. The goat alone now cost more than the price of a cow in the old days. Still Saidi and Chiku did their best. By slowly putting aside the rice Saidi managed to get from his workplace shop now and then, their celebration found them with enough rice to cook for their guests, even though it was of poor quality, since good rice had become so expensive, even in workplace shops, it was now food for the rich and big shots only. Chiku too on her side had done her best and saved the pennies she got from her house door business until she had enough money to buy spices and condiments for seasoning her bottom-grade rice and soft drinks for the children. Given the hard times facing the country, Saidi and Chiku felt they could invite people to their home for an occasion without disgracing themselves.

The invited guests who celebrated the birth of Dogodogo at Saidi's home on Idi day in 1981 were the father and mother of Chiku, Dogodogo's grandparents, Chiku's immediate younger brother with his wife and their two children, and Tabu with her second husband and their three children. Those were the guests who joined Saidi and Chiku with their children and Tabu's children they were bringing up and three other couples, Saidi's neighbors, with their children, about ten in number. And Saidi and Chiku were really happy, because everything went so well! Their guests ate and enjoyed the little there was and everyone praised Chiku for the great cook she was. And although relish had not been quite enough, Chiku was happy and grateful to see that her children and their companions ate with appetite the rice with broth and some greens until they were full and left plenty of food on the serving tray! And each child had two bottles of soda!

Celebrations of that kind are always an occasion for people to meet and chat and for some of them to catch up with each other's news since they last met. And so when the meal was over and the children were enjoying their soft drinks the adults began their palaver, exchanged all sorts of news, their hearts full of happiness and grateful to the Almighty God for giving them life and good health and enabling them to be together with friends and relatives that way.

Regarding their children, Saidi and Chiku appeared to be lucky parents. Even though they had many children and were bringing them up under very difficult conditions, all of them were obedient and well behaved, with the exception of one, their first born daughter, Idaya, who had been a difficult child since she was very young. In the end her parents were convinced that may be it was due to her long illness during her early years, that, without knowing it, they had spoilt her by over-babying her when she was so sick, almost departing form this world, and as a result she became an impossible child. All the same they never gave up on her, never stopped trying to correct her as much as they could. In spite of that she remained a child who quarreled with people and caused trouble at home all the time, with the other children as well as with her parents! At home her mother couldn't ask her to do anything for her, unless she happened to want to. And when in 1979 she finished the seventh grade and was not selected to go to Form 1 of secondary school and became a stay-at-home girl, she became worse! She now wanted to do whatever she liked at home!

That day Idaya had decided not to take part in the celebrations of her family and instead had gone to celebrate the holiday of Idi somewhere else. She came back home when her parents and their relatives and neighbors had finished eating and were continuing their celebrations by their palaver, not to join them, but to show them clearly and in a way they would never forget that her world was completely different from theirs.

To begin with, she had all of a sudden changed so much that her parents and their relatives could not believe it was their daughter they were seeing. Their Idaya entered their house during the gathering of her clan dressed in a very short and really tight-fitting skirt of silky material, the kind of dress she knew her father and mother believed no daughter of theirs dared even think of putting on, and on her feet wearing high-heel "imports" with heels so high that she walked as if she wanted to take off and fly. And, what really made her relatives gape with disbelief, all of a sudden her hair, from whatever chemicals she had put in it, had turned into the hair of some bush-Arab! And her lips were so red you would think she had just sucked the blood of nobody knows what animal! And she was dead drunk! After she entered the house with her wonders she took a folding chair placed against the wall of the sitting room and unfolded it and came to sit right in the middle of the circle of her gathered relatives facing her father, all the while swaying all over the place she almost fell down. And, on sitting down on the chair, her extremely short and tight skirt of silky material was pulled up her body and her thighs were completely exposed! Her father closed his eyes, bent his head and buried his face in his hands. And there and then their daughter let everybody there know that if they thought that was the end of her wonders obviously they didn't know her at all.

"Father, I think we are all here now. Out with your counsel and let's be done with it, so that some of us can attend to business we find more useful," she startled everybody from their confounding disbelief. Throughout the years, every time Saidi celebrated the birth of his child he never failed to talk to his children about the importance of a person's family and clan, of relatives loving each other, and of good behavior. That was an occasion for him to impart to his children the counsel his late father, Mzee Jabiri, left him. That was the family counsel his daughter was sneering at.

"Idaya!" Her mother pleaded with her, her heart pounding and her entire body trembling so much she almost dropped her newborn, Dogodogo, she was holding on her lap during the palaver of the celebrations of her birth.

"Please, Mother! Leave me alone! Children too can have something to say, can't they!"

"My daughter, Idaya! What has happened to you?" her mother continued to try and restrain her before she went too far.

"I said leave me alone, mother, or you didn't hear! Do you perhaps think that we too are overjoyed whenever it dawns to be called and told we should be grateful you have another child? Only you who open your legs for each other enjoy that!"

"God Almighty!" Saidi cried out with shame and sorrow, his head still bent down, not knowing what to do or where to flee to! His daughter was already a grown up woman, and a man in his proper mind doesn't take a cane and beat a female child of his once she reaches puberty. A parent who fails to discipline a child when he or she is still young deserves the shame the child brings him or her later. Those were the thoughts which ran through Ndugu Saidi's mind.

"What is the matter, father!" his daughter took him up on hearing his cry. "What! Did you think we too enjoy the pleasure! Really! Tell me, why should I be grateful I was born in this family? I am your first born daughter, I am seventeen years of age, I am no longer going to school, and I believe I have no bodily defect, I am a woman like any other woman, and I very much desire to get married. But, tell me, the two of you," she continued, all the time shouting at the top of her voice, turning now to face her mother and now her father and pointing a finger at them by turns, "what proper man can desire a woman with *kandambili* flipflops for shoes, who doesn't know how a piece of soap looks like, leave alone powder and perfume, who stinks like rotten fish wherever she passes, and, instead of wearing clothes like other human beings, she is wrapped in tatters like a madwoman! What can possibly make me happy and grateful to see another child born into our home here! Do you perhaps think when you give each other pleasure by opening your legs to each other I too enjoy it?"

"*Aisee!*[41] Idaya! I see you have now gone too far!'" his elder brother, Jabiri, could no longer take it, and stood up and went where she was seated intending to take her out of the house, by force.

"Jabiri, leave her alone, my son. Let your sister say whatever she wants to say, because we don't know who or what set her to it," their father stopped his son Jabiri from confronting his sister.

"Father, you want me to just leave her alone! Allow her to insult our parents in front of us!"

"And you Jabiri shouldn't meddle in matters which don't concern you! If you are happy and content growing up on the fare of *yanga* and salt like a pig, that is your business. Keep on living like a pig until you get a woman also willing to be fed on yanga and salt like a pig, marry her, open each other's legs in your stench of rotten fish and get your houseful of worthless offsprings and stuff them too to bursting with the gruel of *yanga* with salt. That is your own business. But we others can take it no more." She then stood up. Jabiri had gone back to his seat when his father stopped him from dealing with his sister. It now became the turn of his sister to follow him where he was seated. "Come on! Tell the truth, elder brother Jabiri. We must stop lying to ourselves when we know the truth. Don't I look beautiful dressed this way? When you see girls dressed to kill this way, don't you desire them more than a girl with *kandambili* for shoes, her waist in tatters, her stench of rotten fish like that of your sisters in this home of ours wanting to kill you?" She continued vociferating while standing right in the face of his brother and dancing her waist for him. "Tell the truth, brother Jabiri! When a girl passes you by dressed nicely like this and smelling of sweet perfume don't you get aroused?" she continued, putting her bosom very close to her brother's face so that he could smell the sweet perfume she was wearing between her breasts.

"God Almighty!" her father cried again.

Her mother pinched her younger sister Tabu, who was seated next to her, and signaled her to take her daughter away from the sitting room.. If there was one person among her relatives who got on tolerably well with that first born daughter of Chiku, it was her junior mother, her babysitter since she was a little girl, who was more patient with her than her real mother.

Tabu went to where Idaya stood shouting, held her arm and pleaded with her gently, "Idaya, could you please come with me to our room to talk a little."

"You Tabu, don't even dare touch me!" On that day she was no longer "Mama Tabu or Junior Mama." "Take your problems[42] somewhere else, because you and I are in the same boat. You, a woman in your proper mind, went and opened wide your thighs for some worthless male creature who stuck you with a bunch of brats before dumping you with the whole lot of them, and you then lump your brats in your sister's home without any consideration for her when she can't feed her own heap of brats she shits day in day out just so that you could go to look for some other male creatures to open your thighs for and continue to have your lust quenched! *Ntuh!*" she spat on the ground. "I want none of you! I'll have none of you, junior mother or anything! I don't ever want to see you again!"

"My mother!" This time it was her grandmother, the mother of Chiku and Tabu, who cried out, as her two daughters who were being so mercilessly castigated burst out sobbing with tears streaming from their eyes, overwhelmed with sadness.

But even then their daughter was not yet done. "It appears the family palaver this time is mine alone. Very well, because I still have things to tell you, which I think you would like to hear."

The streets of Manzese are always full of people, and on Idi holiday at that hour of the day, they were really crowded. The windows of the sitting room where they were gathered were open, and Ndugu Saidi's daughter was letting her family know what she thought a bout them while shouting louder than a Kariakoo Market auctioneer at work. As a result passers-by had already formed a huge crowd of spectators outside the house who were listening and enjoying the free show.

"Father and mother, you therefore better listen well, so that I can finish what I have to say and go to attend to my business," their daughter continued to broadcast to the crowd from all over Manzese.

"Some of us your daughters are fed up with your daily counsel. We have realized that if we keep listening to the advice of your father, who we others never even saw, who duped you into believing that bearing children is being king on earth when even dogs mount each other and reproduce without being any less dogs, we will continue being stuffed with cheap corn flour and salt like pigs and dressed in the tatters of lepers and, before we know it, find ourselves growing old in this same termite anthill you call a house and die regretting why we were born. We have therefore decided to fend for ourselves. And fortunately we did not need to look far for a teacher. Everyday and every year you our mother who brought us into this world teach us how sweet it is for a woman to open wide her thighs for a man so that he can quench her lust and do for her whatever else she wants. We too are now grown up women. And we too have thighs. Really fresh ones too!"

From the moment she went to show her brother how seductive her waist was when it danced inside a tight-fitting silky dress which left her thighs exposed and to make him smell the sweet perfume on her breasts, she hadn't sat down again, she was still on her feet and pacing about like a sentry on patrol duty. She now held her waist with arms akimbo and turned first to her mother and then to her father, showing them her stomach, "Will you look at me, father and mother! Look at me well! What do you see? Tell me! Aren't you the parents of nine children, or did you perhaps just get them without knowing how they are conceived? Well then, prepare yourselves to welcome two more children to the family of Mzee Saidi son of Jabiri. Yes, one mine and the other one by your beloved daughter, the very same one you sent to the school of the children of the rich and for whom you pay lots of money so that she can go to school all the way to Europe. There she is, fluttering her eyes and pretending to look down ashamed. She doesn't care a damn about shame that one, your Amina. She and I have both got tired of living like pigs, and we are both pregnant."

"Oh dear mother!" This time it was her mother who cried out, and Saidi joined in with "My God!"

Their first born, Jabiri, finished seventh grade in 1977, but wasn't selected to go to secondary school. His parents paid money and arrangements were made and he repeated the seventh grade, twice, still he wasn't selected to enter Form I. He therefore just stayed at home doing nothing, until in 1980 his father finally succeeded in finding him work in his corporation, where he too was hired as a messenger in the same office where his father worked. Idaya herself too did not make it beyond the seventh grade, which she finished in 1979. That was why when their third born, Amina, entered the sixth grade in the same *Uswahilini* primary school in their Manzese to which her elder brother and elder sister had gone, Saidi parted with the money he didn't have and arrangements were made and their daughter was moved to Mlimani Primary School at the University of Dar es Salaam, the school for the children of professors and other important people in the city, which was famous for sending large numbers of its pupils to secondary school every year. That year, 1981, Amina was in the seventh grade at Mlimani Primary, and would at the end of the year sit for the tough national examination which would determine whether she would continue with her education. And it was an open secret that in all the schools renowned for their pupils doing exceptionally well in the examination, the parents of the students paid tuition money every month and their children received additional classes and special preparation for that end-of-primary school examination. So Saidi and Chiku too, in spite of their difficulties in making ends meet, did whatever it took and sent to the University Primary School the monthly fees for the tutors of their daughter Amina, so that at least one of their children would pass the examination and go to secondary school, and by doing so may be open the door of good luck to her younger brothers and sisters when their turns came. That was why Idaya was jealous of her younger sister and saw her as the darling of their parents, since they did not do that for her, their first born daughter.

"What now! What is the matter, father? What is the sad news here? How could the birth of more children, the widening of our clan, be sad news? Since when? Or may be you don't believe me? Ask her, your darling, there she is, if I am lying. Both of us have been fending for ourselves by opening our legs for our white and Arab men[44] on the streets, and we are both pregnant, and very much so. There she is, ask her if I am lying."

There was absolute silence in the gathering of her relatives and neighbors in the sitting room! Each one of them sat with a bent head and a heart weighed down with shame and sadness, as the crowd of Manzese passers-by outside continued to enjoy the free show. With that, their daughter made her exit from the house, walking with her high-heel "imports" as if on springs, wearing sweet perfume on her breasts she didn't mind exhibiting to her brother or father, with her hair of a bush-Arab, and got on her way to look for her black-white and black-Arab men and fend for herself by opening her thighs and waist-dancing for them.

That was how Saidi and Chiku celebrated the birth of their ninth child, Dogodogo, in their *banda* at Manzese.

13

What Idaya broadcast to the whole of Manzese on *Id el fitr* holiday in 1981 just before exiting her parents' house was indeed true. Amina daughter of Saidi, a young girl in the seventh grade at Mlimani Primary School on the campus of the University of Dar es Salaam, her parents' first hope of they too having a child with at least a secondary school education, was pregnant. And likewise her elder sister Idaya herself, who shocked even the hooligans of Manzese by her shameless vociferations in her parents' house that day. And at the end of that year the two of them gave birth, the elder sister first and her sibling two weeks later.

The only thing which remained in doubt was the existence of the two young women's black-white and black-Arab men for whom they were opening their legs while their wealthy lovers in return catered to their every wish and desire. Since their pregnancies became public news until they were admitted to Muhimbili Hospital maternity ward and gave birth and returned to their parents' house with their babies, nobody had ever seen a single one of their black-white men! Not even once! So Ndugu Saidi and his wife Chiku found themselves burdened with yet another responsibility, that of taking care of their grandchildren while continuing to take care of their mothers as well! And unfortunately these new mothers were not like their mother Chiku and other mothers all over the world, who usually love and treasure their newborns when God Almighty blesses them with children. Idaya and her young sister Amina behaved as if the children they gave birth to weren't theirs! As a result Chiku, in addition to what she had to do just to be able to keep her own children from starving to death, now found herself with another difficult task of spending the whole day looking after her infant grandchildren without knowing where their mothers were or where they had passed the night. In December of the following year, the younger sister, Amina, gave birth to her second child. And within no time after that, at the beginning of 1983, the elder sister, the mistress of shocking wonders, Idaya, also gave birth again, and this time to twins. And still not a single one of those black-white men of theirs who were making them bear children without order or plan that way had ever been seen in Ndugu Saidi's home even once!

And while that was happening to Ndugu Saidi in his Manzese home, in Tanzania life was getting worse and worse, in every way and for everybody in the country. And so for the likes of Saidi, low income workers with large families, everything became simply impossible!

A courageous national leader, Prime Minister Ndugu Sokoine, with the indomitable spirit of the legendary Morani warriors of his Masai people, had fought tooth and nail all saboteurs of the national economy, smugglers and black-marketers who hoarded commodities and sold goods at hiked prices, by rounding them up and throwing them in jail for a long time and confiscating their accursed ill-gotten wealth, but all in vain. If anything, the scarcity of food and consumer goods worsened, and where the commodities were found they were sold at real *kuruka* prices! In the end those who had been thrown in jails had to be set free for lack of sufficient evidence of their wrongdoing by the government and they were let loose on the country again, and the out of control hiking of prices their rounding up had triggered became a permanent way of life! The government then came up with a new strategy and allowed *wananchi* with money outside the country to import goods and sell them to their customers at prices they fixed themselves, in the hope that with the availability of goods in large supplies smuggling and price hiking would decline. And indeed, for the first time since nobody knew when, the shops were again overflowing with every kind of goods, among them a commodity which appeared on the market in the country for the first time, and in really big supplies, *mitumba*, clothe-rejects from the dumps of the rich and the dead of Europe and America. Only those imports from abroad proved of no help to ordinary *wananchi* like Saidi. Their prices were so high that they could only feed their eyes on them. Instead of making life easier for *wananchi*, they became a new source of greed and corruption, with everybody trying to sell something on the black market so as to get a bit of money with which to buy those badly needed goods which now temptingly surrounded him or her everywhere. Everybody who could, in Government offices, public corporations, the National Trading Corporation, the National Milling Corporation, the household shops, tried to use his or her position and rank to enrich himself or herself as much as possible. As a result theft, bribery, graft, corruption, hording commodities and price-hiking got really out of hand and the price of everything became outright impossible! Saidi and his family and the masses of poor *wananchi* of Dar es Salaam and the rest of the country found themselves condemned to virtually walking in the streets naked and having to exist on unpalatable corn flour and salt like pigs, day and night, come funerals or weddings!

Idaya and her young sister Amina continued to stay in their father's "anthill" in Manzese, not because they considered it home but only because it was a place to stay free and with a nanny who took care of their children free of charge while they themselves were out on the streets enjoying life. Regarding their life itself, they were now living like bats, going out into the world at night and returning home to sleep during daytime. Both of them were employed as barmaids at

Silent Love Inn bar in Sinza, but the truth was that, like the other barmaids in the city, especially since life in the country became a nightmare, they were love-women at the bar, employed there as bait for the men of means who came to spend freely in a place with plenty of women for love-making to choose from. They did no therefore receive wages at all, even though on paper they were employees of the bar. Their wages were the beer and *konyagi*[45] and roast goat meat the men of pleasure bought them and whatever money they managed to squeeze out of the "black-white men" to whom they sold their bodies. Saidi's two daughters, mothers with babies at home, now went to sleep with men in lodgings all over the city almost every night, except when they were in their monthly periods. They usually did not return to their parents' home until sometime in the morning, and spent the whole daytime sleeping. Then in the evening they dressed nicely and powdered their faces and perfumed and beautified themselves and went to work.

Even though they were now working in that particular way of theirs, Idaya and Amina still did not give a penny to their mother to help her in taking care of their children. She was just their donkey toiling free of charge for them. At best all they did was to buy powdered milk and sugar for the gruel of their babies who hadn't been weaned. Whenever their mother pleaded with them to help her, at least a little, their answer was always, "Who has money to feed the crowd of this house! Whatever you will try to bring home for your children will end up in the bellies of the throng of this house without any of your children ever tasting any of it!"

One morning in 1984, Chiku was busy bathing her last born, Dogodogo, together with her grandchildren, after seeing to it that her children and the children of her sister Tabu who were going to school had all bathed, brushed their teeth, combed their hair and taken their morning fare of *yanga* gruel sweetened with salt. All of a sudden she heard her daughter Idaya shouting, "You dog! Bastard! You lick my sugar, do you know where it came from! Has your father ever brought any of it here even once!"

"Mama, don't beat me! I have stopped, Mama! Sorry, Mama! Don't beat me, Mama!" Then Chiku heard *tu*! *tu*! two successive blows of a heavy stick, and then silence!

Chiku dropped the bowl of water she was using to bathe her children and grandchildren and ran to the room where she heard the commotion, her heart pounding as if her chest wanted to burst. The door of the room was open, and what she saw on getting there was her daughter Idaya holding a heavy piece of wood in one hand and, laying on the ground in front of her and completely still, her first born.

"Idaya, you have killed the child!" Chiku cried out, shaking all over.

"Let him die! Who told him to lick my children's sugar! Has his father ever brought any here even once! Does he even know how he looks like! All the likes of his father know is to impregnate other people's daughters and nothing else, and he dares lick my children's sugar! Today he will simply have to buy me my sugar, unless he dies. So that is why my sugar never lasts, what I buy is at once licked dry by the rabble of brats of this house! I will put an end to it this very day! May be they will lick someone else's sugar, not mine, me Idaya."

Her mother didn't hear a word of what her daughter was blurting out. She was just wailing and screaming, her hands joined behind her head like a person in mourning. The house was at once full of neighbors. Chiku and her neighbors rushed the child to Muhimbili Hospital, only to be told what each and every one of them knew before they even left home, that their child was already dead.

When she went to bathe her children and grandchildren, Chiku started by bathing that child, the eldest of her daughter Idaya's children, a boy who had just turned three. Apparently, as soon as his grandmother finished dressing him in his tiny shirt and pair of shorts and turned to bathing the other children, the boy wondered off into the room of her mother and aunt, Idaya's Room, as everybody called it. Since those two daughters of Saidi and Chiku became mothers, they were given a room of their own and stopped sleeping with the other female children in the Girls Room. That room, which used to be the Visitors Room, since then became known as Idaya's Room, because, of the two sisters, it was the elder who had more rules about the room, especially the one which put it out of bounds to all children in the house.

Every child in that house knew about the sugar in Idaya's cupboard in the room. There wasn't therefore a single child in the house who hadn't filched a bit of her sugar each time she or her sister forgot to padlock the door of their room. Except every child there also knew Idaya's terrible temper and the consequences of messing with anything of hers, and so every time they filched her sugar not only did they make sure they would not be caught but they also took just a little so that it would be difficult for her to realize any had been stolen.

Unfortunately, her son was still too young to know such things. In fact he hadn't even gone to his mother's room that day in search of sugar. He had gone there because on waking up he heard his mother talking with Mama Amina, and that meant she had slept home and was already awake, and he wanted to go to her because he loved his mother like any other child, especially since, even though they lived in the same house, he rarely saw her. It was when he entered the room and didn't see his mother or his aunt anywhere that he remembered there was sugar to lick in there. And when he looked into his mother's cupboard and indeed saw the sugar for the food of his baby twin siblings and the baby of his aunt Amina, he just felt he should do what the other children did all the time. He therefore took the whole bagful of sugar out of the cupboard, sat down, with his back to the open door, stretched out his legs and placed the bag of sugar well on his lap and got busy stuffing sugar into his mouth with both his tiny hands, without the slightest worry in the world!

That is where his mother, who had stepped out for a moment, on coming back to the room found him and killed him on the spot.

There was no case to hear. The accused pleaded guilty to manslaughter and was sentenced to three years in jail. And the following morning the family of Ndugu Saidi made the national headlines. Both the government paper, *Daily News*, and the party one, *Uhuru*, as well as Radio Tanzania, carried the same headline: "ECONOMIC CONDITION OF THE COUNTRY CONTINUES TO WORSEN: MOTHER BEATS TO DEATH CHILD FOR LICKING SUGAR, MANZESE, DAR ES SALAAM!"

That same year of 1984, a few months after his daughter Idaya went to jail, Ndugu Saidi's other daughter, Bibi Ntwara, Bibi as she was called, also gave birth to a child, when she herself was still a child of thirteen years of age! And in the same month in which his child-age daughter came from Muhimbili Hospital with another grandchild for Ndugu Saidi to bring up in his Manzese home, his daughter Amina gave birth inside her parents' very house to her third child.

That is how life was treating Ndugu Saidi of Manzese in the city of Dar es Salaam when he and his son Jabiri were laid off at work in the interest of their nation, as part of the Government's effort to redress the economy by cutting down the cost of running the Government and its public corporations.

PART IV

Ndugu Executive Chairman Nzoka

14

Ndugu Nzoka, the Executive Chairman of the Projects, Wealth, Savings and National Development Corporation, was a Msukuma *mwananchi* who hailed from Bukumbi on the shores of Lake Victoria Nyanza, in Mwanza District of Lake Province of pre-independence days. His official name was now Nzoka Mwanakulanga. And, according to his own account of his life to his children, he was a Tanzanian true patriot who came from far and confronted and overcame a lot of obstacles to get to where he was.

And it was indeed true that Executive Chairman Nzoka had seen a lot in life from the time he was a little boy in his Sukumaland homeland of origin where he and a crowd of his siblings and countless cousins slept in their grandparents' round mud hut which they shared with goats and sheep and calves. When he was taken by his parents to attend school in Mwanza town, every time he came back from vacationing in his native village for a long time the other children at school used to say he smelled of the urine and shit of goats and sheep! But he was now the chief executive officer of the most important and prestigious public corporation in the country, and *mwananchi* who held in his hands a lot of other national responsibilities, and who lived in a mansion fit for a sultan, which he built for himself with his own money in the exclusive residential area of Msasani Peninsula where the real *vizito wananchi* of Dar es Salaam lived.

Ndugu Nzoka was the son of Joni Kulanga son of Petro Nzokayape of Bukumbi, a Msukuma peasant and herder who lived with his father in the same household. As a young boy, he was the most mischievous and unruly child among the countless siblings and cousins he lived with at his grandparents' home, and all that because of being spoilt by his grandmother, who didn't want to hear anybody reprimanding her first born grandson, who was also the first born son of her eldest son, Joni, and who had been named after her husband Nzokayape and likewise baptized with her husband's Christian name of Petro. His father, who wanted his eldest son to get a good education, concluded that if he continued to stay at home with his grandmother, he would never get anywhere in school. "If this son of yours, Petro, goes to school while staying here with his grandfather and grandmother he will end up a goat and cow herder like me his father. He may not even get to the forth grade where I, his ignorant father, ended," Joni told his wife, when their son reached the age of going to school. And so Nzoka was sent to Mwanza town, to his father's brother-in-law, the husband of his paternal aunt, the elder sister of his father, and started school there. His uncle-in-law was a teacher at Mwanza Town Primary School, where a number of his own children were also schooling, and was known for being a no-nonsense teacher.

And indeed his father had predicted right. At his aunt's home, instead of a spoiling grandma, there was nothing but orders for the children, and not obeying an order meant courting trouble. And so Nzoka applied himself really hard to schooling. As a result when he finished forth grade, in 1948, his schooling didn't end there like his father's had. Instead he passed well the Standard V entrance examination and was selected to go to Bwiru Secondary School, the only government secondary school for the entire Lake Province.

Petro found life at Bwiru Secondary School very different from what it was at Mwanza Town Primary School. And among the new things in that important school, and a boarding one to boot, what impressed him most was the "solid rocks" of English, students from the upper classes all the way to Standard X who knew English like Englishmen! And as a result he directed all his energy and mischief of since childhood to learning hard and wanting to know and speak really well the white man's language which distinguished the solid rocks of Standard X from the worthless creatures of Standard V like himself. Both the Headmaster of the school and his assistant were Englishmen, and the Assistant Headmaster, who was also the English teacher for all classes, from Standard V to X, was admired for his mastery of the language. So Petro applied himself really hard to learning the foreign language, including imitating his teacher's pronunciations of his native tongue, all the way to how he contorted his lips in order to articulate well. And not only that: his English teacher walked with one shoulder higher than the other, and the Msukuma boy Petro also began walking as if he was lame in one shoulder. And his efforts paid of really well. In no time he amazed everybody, from his teacher himself to the Headmaster of the school, and even the Standard X rocks themselves, for being a Standard V student who spoke English so well! As a result when he entered Standard VI, though a little boy from the lower classes, he was given special permission by the Headmaster to participate in the debates of the students of the upper classes, Standard VIII to X.

When Petro was recognized for being a special student because of his English, which he spoke better than even those Standard X rocks even though he was still in Standard VI, he decided to change his name and make it sound a bit European. He had entered the school as Petro son of Kulanga, and he now changed his name to Peter John Peterson, that is Peter son of John son of Peter. He therefore became Peter J. Peterson, or P.J. Peterson, or simply Peterson to his Bwiru schoolmates.

He continued being called that until in 1952, when he was in Standard VIII and the fame of Kwame Nkrumah, the warrior son of

Africa who pioneered the struggle for the independence of the African, reached Bwiru Secondary School and every student at the school who was anybody wanted his schoolmates to know that he knew all about that great African politician from West Africa and was already his disciple. From that moment J.P. Peterson decided to use his African names, but by giving them a bit of Nkrumah flavor while making sure they continued to distinguish him for the rock of English he was. He therefore became Nnzokayapeh Kullangahson, by using his clan name, Nzokayape, and his father's name, Kulanga, with appropriate adaptations. It was with the name of Nnzokayapeh Kullangahson that he entered Standard X, in which students took the all important Territorial Standard X Examination of those days.

If there was a single student in the school that year of 1952 who was sure to do well in that difficult examination, it was Nnzokayapeh. His classmates as well as their teachers also shared that conviction, because his relentless hard work was not limited to learning English. He was a young man determined to go far: Makerere College, and then Europe itself. He did not therefore take lightly any single one of his subjects. He was one of three students in their class of twenty-five who were expected to pass with the rare First Class, so difficult to get in that examination that their school had just been hearing about it for many years. And he was so confident of doing well that when he filled in the application form for where he wanted to go after Standard X, he filled in just one place: Standard XI Tabora Secondary School. However, when the results of the examination were out, he passed with Class III!

The examination results angered and confounded Nnzokayapeh Kullangahson beyond measure! Without knowing who to blame, he nevertheless felt he had been grievously wronged and humiliated, especially since his two classmates with whom he had been expected to do well were on their part selected to go to Tabora, even though only one of them had passed with First Class and the other one had been selected to continue with his education by virtue of a good Class II. To make things worse, two more students were selected to go to Tabora even though nobody had expected them to get even that good Class II which made it for them.

That year of 1954 was the year in which Julius Kambarage Nyerere and sixteen fellow *wananchi* founded TANU and plunged *wananchi* of Tanganyika too into the struggle for the liberation of the black man and woman from the yoke of white colonialism, a struggle which had fired up Nzokayapeh since he was still in Standard VIII to the extent of changing his name to make it echo a bit the name of Kwame Nkrumah whose fame had lit that fire in him. At the beginning of 1955, when he was still loitering in Mwanza trying to figure out what do while seething with anger at the whole world for suddenly shattering his entire life by denying him the examination results he needed for continuing with his education, TANU fever was beginning to take hold of Mwanza town. On seeing TANU liberation movement grip the country so powerfully all the way to his Mwanza, the son of Wasukuma peasants decided that in the struggle for the independence of his country was where he could achieve the fame he deserved and due restitution after being unfairly deprived of his right to an education all the way to Europe by the results of the Territorial Standard X Examination. He also decided that the only way to ensure that when he joined TANU he would be given the leadership position a person like him deserved was to join as a proven leader, someone who already had a large following of his own and would bring into the party many new members with him, in other words, a new member who carried some weight.

With that in mind, Nnzokayapeh Kullangahson founded his own association in the town of Mwanza, with even more effort and dedication than he had put into acquiring his exceptional mastery of the language of his country's colonial masters TANU was fighting against. His association was for uniting all the defenseless workers of Mwanza town and surrounding areas: the coolies of Mwanza Port, the bus-boys and lorry-boys of the Indian and Arab owners of buses and trucks in the town, cooks, houseboys, nannies and garden boys of the Indians and Europeans of Mwanza. Recruiting members wasn't easy, especially at the beginning, but Nnzokayapeh was a young man who meant business when he was in pursuit of something he really wanted, and it wasn't long before his association began counting members in hundreds, and then in thousands. He then decided to expand its membership by opening it to milk venders, the sons of the cattle herders of Kayenze and his native Bukumbi and other rural areas around Mwanza, who poured into town daily with their huge cans of milk to sell to the Indians and Europeans and Arabs and hotel and restaurant owners of Mwanza. On the application form for the registration of his association he sent to the Registrar of Societies in Dar es Salaam, Nnzokayapeh called his association for the defense of the weak and helpless: Tanganyika Rural and Urban Laborers Union, TARULA Union in short, to make it clear the association he was founding in Mwanza was meant to be national.

That same year, 1955, when Nnzokayapeh was still waiting for the results of his application for the registration of his association, it was rumored that Nyerere was coming to Mwanza to address a public meeting of *wananchi* on TANU party's struggle for the independence of the African of Tanganyika. He was still determined to recruit many more members for his association and open branches in other parts of the country first before joining TANU, nevertheless he saw that as a great opportunity for him to introduce himself to the founder of TANU and to publicize his association to *wananchi*, especially since he himself couldn't convene public meetings before his association was registered. And so, without saying a word to the local TANU party leaders in Mwanza, he prepared his followers for participating in the public meeting of the president of TANU determined to make a real impression.

And indeed on the day Julius Kambarage Nyerere, the President of TANU Party, addressed the public rally in Mwanza, the members of TARULA Union participated in the rally in an unforgettable way. First two TANU party leaders from Mwanza spoke, before a third one took over to welcome their guest speaker, the leader of the party for the liberation of the people of Tanganyika, to address *wananchi* of Mwanza. Before Honorable Nyerere got up from his seat on the dignitaries' platform, Nnzokayapeh and all the members of his association stood up. All were distinguishable by the white piece of cloth each one of them wore across the shoulders like Wasukuma Bucheyeki dancers. Nnzokayapeh had prepared well for the moment and his group had been sitting right at the foot of the dignitaries' platform. Nnzokayapeh himself, in addition to the white toga, also wore across each shoulder a broad belt decorated with beads he had borrowed from a famous lead-singer of a dance group in his native Bukumbi.

As Nyerere was about to stand up, before he was on his feet Nnzokayapeh was hoisted up high on the shoulders of one of his followers, right in front of the dignitaries' platform. Nyerere had therefore to wait for that Msukuma lead-singer to finish his part, believing that to be part of the reception program his Mwanza hosts had prepared for him. There and then, as if by the moment of hesitation he showed the President of TANU Party was inviting him, Nnzokayapeh jumped onto the platform an took the microphone! "Honorable Mwalimu Nyerere, President of the Glorious TANU Party, my name is Nnzokayapeh Kullangahson. I come from Bukumbi, in this District of Mwanza. I am the Secretary General of the Tanganyika Rural and Urban Laborers Union, TARULA Union for short, the association for defending the rights of defenseless workers employed by exploitative colonial masters. Therefore we the members of TARULA Union would like to welcome you, the Most Most Honorable Mwalimu Nyerere, President of the Glorious TANU Party in combat for the liberation of black people from the yoke of British colonialism so that we may regain our freedom and full rights as human beings, to our Mwanza with the traditional song we Wasukuma sing to welcome the head of a household returning home from a distant journey, called 'Father of the Household'." And, in spite of all he had done to imitate the English, Nnzokayapeh was nonetheless a true Msukuma young man, born and bred, well versed in the traditions of his people. And he turned into a real Msukuma dance group lead-singer on the dignitaries' platform. The song he had chosen for his followers for welcoming Honorable Nyerere was known to Wasukuma from almost every corner of Sukumaland, and when the members of his group followed his lead and sang with him virtually the entire huge crowd at the rally turned into a mass choir which burst open the sky with one voice. Everybody, including the local TANU leaders and organizers of the rally, joined in the song. As a result, when people dispersed at the end of the meeting most of them went away talking about the participation of Nnzokayapeh instead of what the President of TANU they had come to listen to had said.

From that day in 1955, Nyerere did not have a more dedicated and hard working party assistant than that Msukuma young man.

After the rally Nyerere told his hosts in Mwanza to find and bring to him the young man who had fired up that way the masses at the rally, and the two had a very long talk together. And in the course of their discussions, now in English and now in Swahili, as educated *wananchi* used to do in those days, Nyerere was equally amazed at how well that young man with a mere Standard X education spoke

English, and yet he himself was highly educated, all the way to Great Britain itself, and among the African leaders known for speaking the white man's language very well. Nyerere was equally impressed by the young man's knowledge of every kind of event which mattered in the country and the world, even though he had gone to school at Bwiru in the same Mwanza District he came from and beyond which he had never traveled even once, not even to go to some other parts of the country, leave alone abroad! Nyerere was further amazed by the wonders the young man performed at the rally, after Nnzokayapeh had told him the real reason behind what he did and what he meant to achieve by it! There and then Nyerere decided that the young man would be ideal for the propagation and strengthening of the party in the country. Nnzokayapeh too on his part, on seeing the great leader of TANU clearly recognizing that he, Nnzokayapeh Kullangahson, was a very intelligent person with unique and special talents, there and then decided he would work for the leader of TANU to the best of his ability, in whatever he asked him to do. As a result Nyerere hired the Msukuma young man as his party assistant, who would move to Dar es Salaam party headquarters as soon as arrangements for him to move were completed.

That too was the day the young Msukuma changed his name again, to Nzoka Mwanakulanga. Nyerere lectured him that calling himself Kullangahson was evidence of a colonial mentality totally unacceptable in a leader of the liberation struggle of *wananchi*. "We too went through that, my dear young man, so nobody can laugh at anybody here. Take me for example, when I was a real slave of the colonial mentality, I wanted my name Kambarage, a good name with an important meaning in the language of my Wazanaki people, to be Cambridge! And no joke! Really Cambridge! And I felt really proud when I was called Julius Cambridge! No joke at all!" Nyerere himself was the first to burst out laughing really loud, with his dear young man following suit. And from that day Nnzokayapeh Kullangahson became Nzokayape Mwanakulanga, which means Nzokayape son of Kulanga in his native Kisukuma language. And because Nzokayape means "white snake" in Kisukuma, he shortened that name by dropping "yape" from it, in case it were mistaken for a sign of black people's colonial mentality of adoring the whites and everything white. He therefore now became Nzoka Mwanakulanga.

Nzoka now became a TANU leader and a famous one too. And not because of the strange way he joined the party, but on real merit. Regarding his own association, TARULA Union, his application for the registration of the association was denied. The colonial government had already decided to clamp down on every kind of struggle for the rights of *wananchi* in Sukumaland. He had therefore sent in his application at the wrong time. One of the restrictions the colonial government had imposed on TANU party was to require that every branch the party opened be registered as a new and different association, so as to be able to disrupt the activities of the party fighting for the liberation of *wananchi* by denying its new branches registration or closing the branches it didn't like while still claiming it hadn't banned the party itself. *Wasukuma* had bitter grievances against the colonial government at the time. The colonial government had imposed on them, a people for whom herding cattle is the principal occupation, cattle tax for every head of cattle they owned, even though they were also paying capital tax like everyone in the rest of the country. In addition to that, the government had also ordered them to reduce by ten percent their herds by selling their cattle at a give away price to a colonial company, Tanganyika Packers. Because TANU was trying to defend *wananchi* of *Sukuma* land against such injustice, the colonial government decided to ban the party in the whole region. As a result every time the party applied for the registration of a new branch in Sukumaland, the application was denied. From Shinyanga to Geita, Malampaka, Nassa, and Nera, in all those places TANU was denied permission to open new branches. And Nyerere entrusted the task of spreading the party in those areas of Sukumaland which could not be reached through official party branches to his dynamic young man he had just discovered in the region. And Nzoka Mwanakulanga carried on his task of spreading the party in the region by underground means with such energy and resolve that some of the places he operated in within no time had more TANU members than many registered party branches in the country.

Mwalimu Nyerere was thrilled by what his young man, Nzoka, accomplished in Sukumaland. As a result when at the end of 1956 he moved to the party headquarters in Dar es Salaam, at the time when Saidi son of Jabiri had also just been hired there, he at once became the most trusted and beloved assistant to the President of TANU Party, entrusted with great responsibilities and on whom the party president relied a lot. And Nzoka Mwanakulanga continued to serve the leader of TANU with his characteristic boundless effort of since his school days. He became Nyerere's assistant and disciple who imitated how his leader spoke Swahili, how he laughed, and who too walked with a miniature black knobkerrie stuck under an armpit as his leader used to do in those days of the struggle for independence. And he continued working for his leader with the same zeal until the 9th of December, 1961, when *wananchi* of Tanganyika won their independence through their TANU Party.

15

Only one month had passed since independence when *wananchi* in the whole of Tanganyika as well as their friends from all over the world were shocked by the announcement that the Most Most Honorable Julius Kambarage Nyerere, the President of TANU Party which had freed *wananchi* of Tanganyika by giving them their *Uhuru*, was resigning from his position as the first Prime Minister of independent Tanganyika! However, Mwalimu Nyerere had not fought for the independence of *wananchi* of Tanganyika because he wanted rank. Rank is a surety-bond entrusted to the leader by the people he or she represents. And Mwalimu Nyerere was convinced that the masses of the peasants and workers of Tanganyika needed him more for the task of better propagating and establishing their party and its policies in the country, so as to properly prepare their young nation for the difficult undertaking of building the nation through self-reliance and of defending their independence. He therefore let another TANU leader, Rashidi Kawawa, take over the position of Prime Minister, so that he would dedicate all his efforts to the political organization and education of *wananchi* and *wazalendo* of their young nation. On the same day he announced his resignation, Mwalimu Nyerere called Nzoka to his office, at the headquarters of TANU on Lumumba Street. Nzoka went into the office ready to receive the instructions of how he was to help Mwalimu with the task of politically strengthening the nation. Mwalimu however wasn't calling him for that.

"Nzoka, I want you to prepare yourself for another national leadership task, a much more difficult one, that of national construction, that is the development of our country's economy and its social services, which is by far a more difficult undertaking than the struggle which won us our independence, which is still nothing but flag independence. It is the development of our nation, economically and socially, which will turn our flag independence into real independence.

"I would have very much liked to have you help me with the strengthening of the party in the country, but I want you to take this opportunity to further your education and to travel a bit and see the world, so that you know what today's world is like. A leader with limited education and a narrow understanding of the world we live in cannot be a good national leader of his people. And I want you to know that, when I resume heading our government, should *wananchi* continue to want my leadership, I will come back as the President of the Republic of Tanganyika. An independent country which is under a colonial Governor General and continues to recognize the Queen of England as its Head of State is unacceptable to *wananchi*, and also to me personally as well as to all the freedom fighters of the world. And the construction of the Republic of Tanganyika will require solid and dynamic TANU leaders like you, resolute sons and daughters of TANU who know what they are doing. And leadership of that kind requires very sound formation. And I would like you to avoid the example of some people who announce to the public they are going to study for I don't know what qualification when they go abroad. Because if you do that and then come back empty handed, without the qualification, then to the people you have failed, in other words you are not intelligent. And, Nzoka, let's admit it, whether we like it or not, lack of intelligence is not a good qualification for a leader."

Ndugu Nzoka, who for a long time had been claiming he was the one who gave Nyerere the name Mwalimu when he called him by that name for the first time at a public rally in Mwanza in 1955, became therefore the first person to know Mwalimu was preparing Tanganyika to become a republic. And at the beginning of 1962 he set out to educate himself in preparation for the task Mwalimu promised him, of being part of the leadership team of their Republic. And right away he went first to Ghana, to see with his own eyes the country of his hero who introduced him to what politics was all about, Dr. Kwame Nkrumah, the veteran of African liberation struggle. In Ghana he took a two-month course in Political Science and Leadership at Winneba Nkwame Nkrumah Institute, the institute of Osagyefo Dr. Kwame Nkrumah's Convention People's Party, which had made Ghana the first African country to liberate itself from the yoke of the white colonialism by leading the country to its independence in 1957. On returning to Dar es Salaam, before he had settled back he got an invitation to study Political Science and Economics in Israel and take a study tour of the country. Before the Jews invaded Arab countries in 1967, Israel was seen by many African countries as a young nation which was making rapid progress and therefore from which they could learn a lot. In Israel he chose to study the Economics of Developing Countries, for three months. He had just returned home when he left for another study trip abroad, this time at the invitation of yesterday's colonial rulers of Tanganyika, the British, through the British Council, to go to Europe where he had desired to go since he was at Bwiru Secondary School. In Europe he took again the same subjects he considered most relevant to his work as a national leader of his country, Economics and Political Science, at Ruskin College, the adult education institute of Oxford University.

When Nzoka came back home from England it was the end of 1962, and the country was in the midst of the campaign for the election of the first president of the Republic of Tanganyika. And, as usual, he got down to campaigning really hard for his leader, Mwalimu Nyerere. As a result Mwalimu Nyerere was elected by *wananchi* of Tanganyika to be their first President with a resounding victory. On the 9th of December, in 1992, the first anniversary of the independence of Tanganyika, Mwalimu Nyerere moved into the Residence of the Governors of the Kings and Queens of Great Britain as the first President of his country. And on the same day, before he had even announced his Cabinet, Mwalimu appointed Nzoka Mwanakulanga Advisor to the President for Internal Affairs and Politics.

His work in *Ikulu* proved to be yet another opportunity for Nzoka to continue enhancing his education. His new job as the President's adviser did not require his presence in his office all the time. There were no less than five other advisers to the President and, even though each one of them headed a different department, still their work of advising the President was of a kind where any one of them could fill in for an absent fellow adviser. Moreover Mwalimu was still urging the young man, his dynamic assistant of so many years, to continue educating himself so that he could assume positions of greater responsibility in the country. And in 1963, Nzoka, who was perceptive enough to see that Mwalimu Nyerere was ideologically already leaning towards socialism, decided to go to socialist Europe to see how a socialist society looked like, after he had seen what capitalist Europe was all about, and went to Russia, to Lumumba University, which had been specially built by that country for the education and formation of skilled manpower and leaders of developing countries like Tanganyika. He stayed in Russia for more than a year and a half, busy studying Economic Planning, Socialist Ideology, and Russian language. Then, at the end of 1964, he came back home for a bit of vacation. In the following year, 1965, he worked in his office for just a while before going on yet another British Council study trip, to the same British institute he went to before, Ruskin College, where he took the same subjects he took there in 1962, this time at a higher level, for a period of three months. After that he went to study at another institute in the country, the renowned Development Studies Institute of the University of Sussex. He returned home in the middle of 1966. In the same year, in September, he set out on yet another trip abroad, this time at the invitation of the American government, to go and study for four months at one of the most prestigious universities in that country, Harvard, where he took a course in Trade-Union Leadership. In America he saw with his own eyes what development meant in that bastion of economic imperialism in the world. He returned home in January 1967. The following month, February 1967, the Arusha Declaration was proclaimed and the *Ujamaa* era of Tanzania was launched.

One morning, on a Monday, two weeks after the proclamation of the Arusha Declaration, President Nyerere called Nzoka to his office in *Ikulu*.

"Nzoka, I am glad to see that you have done your best to advance your education. I have gone through your personal file carefully, and it is obvious that you chose your courses intelligently whenever you got an opportunity to go to study abroad. I was particularly pleased with your decision to go to study in Russia as well, since by adopting the Arusha Declaration we have decided to develop a socialist society in Tanzania, and the source and stronghold of socialism in today's world is Russia. In short, I am convinced that the courses of study and the experience you gained from all over the world over the years have prepared you very well for assuming the responsibilities I want to entrust you with.

"As you know, on nationalizing the pillars of our national economy in accordance with the Arusha Declaration we have decided to establish public corporations to manage those levers of the economy of our country. The public corporation the country will depend on most in that undertaking is the Projects, Wealth, Savings and National Development Corporation. I am appointing you the Executive Chairman of that very important public corporation."

Nzoka Mwanakulanga's heart pounded so much out of happiness that his ears were blocked. When thanking Mwalimu Nyerere he heard his voice sounding from very far as if someone else instead of he was speaking. "Mwalimu, I thank you very much, my Mzee. And I will strive to the best of my ability to merit this great honor you have conferred on me."

"Very well, Nzoka. Only you must always remember that for us leaders of the people rank is a surety-bond we hold on behalf of the public so that we can work for the benefit of *wananchi*. So please don't imagine, even for a day, that this job is yours by right or a job I have personally given you. I don't have a job, not even a single one, which is mine to give as I like. I am nothing but a representative of the people of this nation. It is in that capacity that I find you to be a leader with the needed qualifications for running this important vehicle for the development of our society I am entrusting you with. And always remember the fact that you serve the people and not the rank you hold or Mwalimu Nyerere. If you bear that in mind all the time, you will never stray from the right path in the execution of your duties."

And with those words Mwalimu Nyerere bestowed on Nzoka Mwanakulanga that big post with its many responsibilities.

16

For those who knew Ndugu Nzoka Mwanakulanga and Ndugu Saidi son of Jabiri, there was nothing surprising when Nzoka, on being entrusted by Mwalimu Nyerere with the responsibility of running that very important public corporation, he on his part chose Saidi to be the Head Messenger of his corporation. From the time they were at the Party Headquarters on Lumumba Street, where both were hired in 1956, to when they worked in *Ikulu* where they had been transferred at the same time in 1962, Saidi and Nzoka were really great friends, to the extent that many people thought they were blood relatives. When Nzoka arrived in Dar es Salaam from upcountry he first stayed at Saidi's in Kariakoo. They even married at the same time, like two brothers who had decided to get married together, because when Saidi got married, in 1962, shortly after the two friends were transferred to *Ikulu*, two months later Nzoka went home to Sukumaland and he too got married. And when Nzoka arrived in Dar es Salaam with his bride, it was Saidi and his wife Chiku who welcomed the newlyweds in the city and held a reception for them. And from that moment the friendship of the two men was further cemented by the friendship of their wives.

For Nzoka and other *wananchi* with big posts, part of the fruits of independence was living in Oyster Bay "White-town", the former European residential district of Dar es Salaam, where before independence the only African who stepped there was the cook, the nanny, the houseboy and garden-boy of the whites. In spite of that, most of the African elite now living in White-town, especially their wives, continued to have very close relationships with their fellow *wananchi* of *Uswahilini*, where most of their relatives and friends in the city lived. When Nzoka too brought into the city his bride, whose name was Beatrice, Bea for short, Chiku, the wife of Saidi, a young woman like herself, the wife of her husband's friend who welcomed her into that big city she had never been to but where Chiku was born and therefore a place in which she knew everything which mattered, and a kind and very generous woman to boot, became Bea's closest friend. As a result, since living in her own home in the city Bea never left Oyster Bay to go to the market in Kariakoo without calling at Chiku's so that Chiku could accompany her, never went shopping in India-town without Chiku, and, because there weren't African women hair stylists in Oyster Bay, never went to have her hair done without Chiku accompanying her to the hair saloons of her Kariakoo neighbors. And with their wives spending so much time together, Nzoka and Saidi became even greater friends.

Saidi' wife was the first to give birth to her first born, Jabiri. But in that same year, 1963, Bea too gave birth to her first child, whom her husband decided to call Mayala, the name of his paternal great-grandfather. And then Bea began giving birth without pause, the kind of child bearing Grandma Ntwara didn't approve, so that by 1967, when Chiku gave birth to her third child, Bea was already expecting her fifth. And Bea's caretaker throughout those years she was giving birth to children without a moment of rest was none other than Chiku, irrespective of whether she too was expecting or nursing her own newborn. And because that was also the time Nzoka was traveling abroad without rest to further his education, Saidi found himself having to look after two homes, his own in *Uswahilini* of Kariakoo and his friend Nzoka's in White-town, Oyster Bay. In fact, it was as if Nzoka came on vacation from his endless travels in Russia and America and England and everywhere in the world just in order to impregnate his wife Bea with yet another child and then left all the responsibility of taking care of his pregnant wife and the new mother and her newly born baby to Saidi and his wife Chiku.

And that was how things remained between the two friends, until Mwalimu Nyerere appointed Ndugu Nzoka Executive Chairman of that all important public corporation.

Saidi was the first to notice the change of behavior in his friend Nzoka. All the time they had worked together, from TANU Headquarters to *Ikulu*, his friend Nzoka had always been his superior at work. He wasn't therefore working under him for the first time. Except this time Nzoka wasn't any longer his workplace superior he always knew, a great friend of his and a die-hard believer in the ideology of TANU and its leader, Mwalimu Nyerere, which emphasized the equality of all human beings and recognized the importance and necessity of all work, from the smallest to the biggest, and the need to respect all work equally. All of a sudden it was as if Nzoka had grown wings and wanted to fly and go and live in the sky, stop living with his fellow human beings on this earth! At work, instead of being a leader who supervised and gave directions to fellow workers, he was driving his employees like the colonial Bwana Tumbo Tumbo and treating them with the contempt of an Indian master for his houseboy! And that too was how he treated Saidi, his friend of so many years! But still Saidi saw all that as of no concern to him. If he wanted their friendship to continue, that was well and fine with him. If he now wanted him to be nothing to him but his messenger, that too was just fine. And may be he appeared that way because he was overwhelmed by work at his new job with its numerous big responsibilities. For it was still true that bringing him to his corporation and making him Head Messenger with a starting salary of more than twice what he was getting in *Ikulu* was an honor to him and proof of true friendship for everybody to see. Who but a true friend would do that for a person without education like him Saidi! He therefore continued serving him without any complaint, even when his friend made it clear to him he didn't want him to show that they knew each other except as a messenger and his employer, by not exchanging greetings with him when they met or even when he called him to his office to give him work. Even when he stopped altogether coming to his home in Kariakoo, Saidi continued to think well of him and to be grateful to him for all the good things he had done for him.

Those public corporations which were born in a single day with the Arusha Declaration appeared in the life of *wananchi* of Tanzania with a real bang, especially in Dar es Salaam, where almost all of them were a headquartered. To begin with, its employees, especially those holding top ranks, hundreds of all kinds of managers, had very good salaries, in addition to many other fringe benefits. As a result, even though *Naizesheni*[46] started with independence, the real *Naizesheni* was ushered in by the army of managers of the public corporations created in the wake of the proclamation of the Arusha Declaration.

Those were the real black-whites! Especially those with the title of General Manager or Executive Chairman, positions to which a person was appointed by the President of the Republic, Mwalimu Nyerere himself, positions of real power and money, and whose beneficiaries were accountable to nobody else except Mwalimu Nyerere alone! And in the whole of Dar es Salaam, among all those *Naizesheni*, no man was more *kizito* than Ndugu Executive Chairman Nzoka Mwanakulanga, the Executive Chairman of the Projects, Wealth, Savings and National Development Corporation.

And indeed Ndugu Nzoka Mwanakulanga became a famous personage in the city. And among the things he was best known for was his love for women and addiction to sex. As part of that fame of his was the claim by some women that if a woman made the mistake of asking for a lift from that Executive Chairman, she had better know that as soon as she entered his car, even if it was in the morning hours and she was going to work, he would not stop the car until he got to Bahari Beach Hotel, where that *kizito* had a room reserved for him every day for that particular function. There were some women who even claimed that if a beautiful young woman made the mistake of entering his office, even if it was in the middle of work hours, she must count herself really lucky to come out safely. In spite of that, all the women who counted themselves real women in the city agreed on finding one thing really good about him, which was that the woman who was lucky enough to be loved by Executive Chairman Nzoka lacked nothing again in this world! That she would have all the money, clothes, shoes, or whatever else she may desire! And that was what Rose-Mary too heard.

Rose-Mary was a young Mchaga woman from Kilimanjaro. She completed Standard XII in 1966 at the most famous secondary school for women in the country at the time, Tabora Girls Secondary School. She passed very well her end of secondary school examination and was selected for further education, but she chose not to continue with schooling. Instead she descended to Dar es Salaam and plunged into offices in the city in search of work. She was hired by one of the imperialist multinational corporations which on being nationalized in 1967 were taken over by the Projects, Wealth, Savings and National Development Corporation. Because it was Rose-Mary's company building which became the headquarters of Ndugu Executive Chairman Nzoka's new public corporation, Rose-Mary worked in Ndugu Nzoka's office building.

In those days Standard XII was still considered a good education. And, on the part of women, a young woman who had completed Standard XII was seen as a highly educated woman. But Rose-Mary wasn't just an educated woman. Indeed that wasn't her greatest attribute, even though it too counted. Rose-Mary was simply blessed to be born a woman who eclipsed in beauty all the other women around her wherever she happened to be, ever since she was a child. It was said that her mother was Mmasai and it was her father who was Mchaga, and what the mixture of Mmasai and Mchaga produced was a woman of rare beauty, with the body of Mmasai maiden, tall, soft and slender with a silk-smooth skin and the long neck of a giraffe, and the light complexion of Mchaga beauty! That was Rose-Mary who was working in Executive Chairman Nzoka's office building. And from the very first day he laid eyes on her, Ndugu Executive Chairman Nzoka had no doubt at all that God created that young woman for him.

Rose-Mary, as beautiful as she was and in spite of her age of a young woman who had completed Standard XII, was still a virgin. At the school where she came from as well as back home in Kilimanjaro and in the city of Dar es Salaam, many of her friends who were not yet married had either got pregnant and already had children or had aborted pregnancies. Even those who hadn't experienced any of that had at least a boyfriend. She had no boyfriend and never had any, not even one. Her answer to herself every time men wanted her or women friends of hers tried to convince her to follow their example was only one: "With me the man who will deprive me of my virginity must climb on me at the cost of diamonds!" And the more she grew up and matured into a young woman who knew what was going on in the world and understood perfectly well the meaning of the way men of every kind looked at her everywhere she went the more she was convinced that the man with her diamonds was bound to come to her. And the day she laid her eyes for the first time on the young Executive Chairman of their new corporation, the greatest *Naizesheni* in the whole of Tanzania, she decided, before she even heard of his reputation with women, that he was the man with her diamonds. And when she heard of his fame, she became absolutely sure that he was bound to give her the diamonds. All of them!

Rose-Mary's turn to be loved by the Executive Chairman of their corporation came on a Saturday. The Executive Chairman told his secretary he wanted to see the young woman in his office after work. Saturday was a half workday and employees went home at half past noon. And at exactly half past twelve noon that young woman knocked at the door of the office of the secretary of the chief executive officer of their corporation. The secretary of the Executive Chairman let the young woman in, and then pressed a button on the telephone and informed the Chairman that his guest had arrived, her heart full of sadness and sorrow at the thought of what she knew awaited that daughter of some parents, so beautiful and as young as her own daughters, inside the office of her boss. She was the very first woman to go through hell in that office, on the visitors' couches, even though she was the wife of a self-respecting husband with a high ranking job and a mother with grownup children who respected her a lot. Her consolation on her part was to say to herself that she had to put up with it, since from the day she was the victim of the despicable deeds of her Chairman in that office she was never again short of petty cash and money for whatever she needed, leave alone the fact that her salary, which was already good, was immediately increased threefold. And so if she was a shameful wife and mother, so be it! Whatever the case her husband, a real African man, was bound to have lots of other women, even though she had never seen or heard of him cheating on her. And as to her children, they were the reason why she had to struggle to the extent of soiling her character and disgracing herself that way. With her mind full of such thoughts, she opened the door of the office of her boss for Rose-Mary to go in. That was an important part of her work, almost daily. What was more, she too, from time to

111

time, still took turns at entertaining her boss by catering to his dirty doings, especially when they went together on official trips upcountry or abroad. So, as soon as she handed over to her boss his guest, she took her handbag and closed her office and got on her way back home to her husband and children and left that daughter of some dear parents to her turn of dealing with the world of Ndugu Executive Chairman Nzoka.

Inside the office things heated up right away. They were seated on a bed-like couch, big and long, and it didn't take long for Rose-Mary, after she had sipped this and that soda, tasted sweet and sour wine, heard an aspect of her beauty whispered in one of her ears and another one in the other ear, to consent to sit on the lap of her boss. Since the day the young woman decided that the Executive Chairman of their corporation was the man with diamonds for her, she came to work daily fully prepared for the opportunity which now was finally hers. And so when she allowed herself to be placed on the lap of her corporation Chairman, she kept limply rolling her soft body this way and that way against the chest of the man cradling her, before allowing him to undo the buttons on the upper part of her dress. She had no bra on and her breasts of Mmasai maiden stood firm and erect on her bosom like spears, red and full like ripe tomatoes! The young woman pretended she was shocked at being undressed that way and made a slight start and in so doing dropped her breasts in the mouth of her corporation Chairman. Ndugu Executive Chairman Nzoka swore he had never encountered a woman with such hot breasts in this world! When Rose-Mary was informed her Executive Chairman wanted her, she prepared herself for the visit by spraying some maddeningly sweet perfume in between her breasts. The result of that sweet perfume compounding with the hot naked bosom of a young woman with a body as soft as silk was to make Ndugu Executive Chairman Nzoka lose his mind altogether! He no longer knew what he was saying or promising as he kissed the young beautiful woman's breasts like a man possessed. But when he tried to go further and open all the buttons on her dress, which was split from top to bottom in front, so as to kiss her whole body until he sacrificed himself to it by entering her, Rose-Mary held his hand and stopped him: "No, Mzee! I am afraid."

"Afraid of what, my Rose-Mary? What is new here?"

"I have never done those things, Mzee."

"Even if you have never done it, every woman has her first time. Every one has his or her first time. Even I had my first time!"

"I am afraid, Mzee."

In Sukumaland where Executive Chairman Nzoka came from, on the first time a woman would never let a man make love to her until he had toiled for it, irrespective of how much she loved him or whether she was a confirmed tramp or a maiden. A man had first to prove to the woman that he was a real man, by overpowering her! Only then would the woman allow him to enter her body. Even in the case of one's wife. He, Nzoka, still remembered his wrestling match with his wife Bea on their first night, in spite of the fact that they were already married in church and, what was more, even though his Bea was anything but a virgin when they married. "May be that is how things are among the Wachaga too," Chairman Nzoka made up his mind. "And, at any rate, don't we see all the time women, from maidens to people's wives, pretend to say no when in fact all they are doing is playing hard to get," he summed up his thoughts, as the body of the young woman in his hands continued to drive him crazy. With that conviction, all the remaining buttons on Rose Mary's dress flew off in a single stroke.

"Mzee, you are tearing my dress!"

"Who cares about a dress you girl! You can have all the clothe-shops in the whole of Dar es Salaam if you want. All you have to do is to be nice to your Mzee."

Rose-Mary was now really frightened. In spite of having prepared herself for many days to make that Mzee of hers really love-crazy the day she would get her chance to be alone with him face to face, she was now really scared of what could happen to her! Nzoka Mwanakulanga, his powerful position notwithstanding, was still a child of Wasukuma herders, who grew up grazing cattle the whole day long in pasturelands where wrestling, and even stick-fighting, was an ordinary game for young boys while looking after their animals. It therefore required hardly any effort for him to pin down the young woman lying on her back on that bed-like couch of an office inherited from an imperialist business firm. After that it was jus a matter of Ndugu Executive Chairman Nzoka coiling his right leg on the left leg of the soft body of the Mchaga beauty, like a python securing a goat in its coils before swallowing it, and then tightening his leg-hold just a little for the young woman with breasts which burnt a man's body like cooking-stones from which a boiling pot had just been lifted to cry out in real pain! Then her slip and panties were torn off her body like pieces of paper. Now Rose-Mary cried and wept in earnest: "Yesuu! Lord Yessuu! God Almighty! Yessu and Mary! I am dying, oh God! Mother, I am dying!.....," she whimpered in her Kichaga-Swahili accent, without however crying out loud or shouting for help! To Chairman Nzoka his beautiful companion weeping and crying quietly that way meant she was signaling and welcoming him into her, in spite of pretending to resist.

Rose-Mary was indeed still a virgin. And by Ndugu Executive Chairman Nzoka entering her roughly and forcefully that way, as if he was wrestling a fellow Msukuma herder, he tore and wounded her very badly! Blood from the loss of her virginity and from the wound of that terrible tear had formed a pool on the couch and Rose-Mary was now crying from the pain of her wounds. Executive Chairman

Nzoka, with the demon in him exorcised, had come to his senses and was now in the midst of a different hustle, soothing and cajoling the young beauty he was again cuddling on his lap while wiping her tears with endless kisses and promising her everything on earth. The young woman finally stopped crying and coiled up on the chest of her corporation Chairman, completely quiet, like a baby who had cried to exhaustion and fallen asleep!

In those early years of their country's independence, in general, things were really great for *wananchi* of Tanzania. The economy of their country was expanding, and the social services they had been promised by their political leaders during the struggle for independence were no longer just promises but real deeds people were witnessing. Those years of prosperity were also, for the country's Government and the Party leaders, a time when public celebrations were held for every national event which deserved commemorating. It was a time when in Dar es Salaam throughout the year big and lavish parties with plenty of free food and drinks accompanied by the music of the famous bands of the city were thrown in celebration of this or that occasion in the Diamond Jubilee Hall, the Arnatouglu Hall, the Institute of Adult Education Hall and the halls of all the big hotels in the city. To our national leaders, those festivities were considered part and parcel of official business. As a result many of them judged it more appropriate to go to those rumbas with partners from their workplaces instead of their wives. And for many of them those workplace partners of theirs were their secretaries or other young women from their offices who were fit companions for a man in a leadership position in the gathering of fellow leaders. And Ndugu Executive Chairman Nzoka had decided, since the very first day he laid eyes on Rose-Mary in his office building, that she would now be his party partner from work. A young woman who would make a man put his colleagues in their proper places. " A woman who, when she accompanies you to a party, as soon as you arrive at the door causes a quarrel between men and their partners! Every man in the entire hall stops looking at his partner or at any other woman whatsoever by as much as a single glance, the eyes of each and every man glued on your partner alone!" And that was the young woman he was now holding in his arms as she slept all quiet and peaceful like an infant!

Because he intended to make the young woman his official party-partner, Chairman Nzoka already had a special program in place for her, for that day and afterwards. And, as part of that program, he had given orders for the Head Messenger of the Corporation, Ndugu Saidi son of Jabiri, not to go home until told, even though there were two other messengers already scheduled to remain on duty after work-hours that day.

In this world, every one of us has his or her way of understanding other people. And we are usually convinced that what we think of other people is what they actually are. Chairman Nzoka was likewise convinced he knew all about his Head Messenger, Saidi son of Jabiri, from beginning to end, even though Saidi himself had never, even once, told him the real story of his life, because he was not a person to divulge the secrets of his life to those they didn't concern. And to Saidi the secrets of his life concerned only his wife Chiku and their children. His boss was however certain that if in this world there was a single person who when told to do anything by his superior at work he did it without ever grumbling or asking a question, that person was his Head Messenger, with whom he had worked for over a decade and who had therefore no secrets for him. That was his understanding of Ndugu Saidi. In fact that was the real reason why he hired him as the Head Messenger of his corporation.

That day Executive Chairman Nzoka had ordered Ndugu Saidi to remain at work so that, after his doings with the young woman in his office, Saidi would escort her to where she lived and know the place. And from there on he would be his one and only emissary and confidant in his relationship with the young woman who was to be his companion at official parties in the city. And that was what Executive Chairman Nzoka right away told his Head Messenger when he called him to his office, after matters in there had cooled down sufficiently.

Executive Chairman Nzoka had now moved to a love-seat beside the couch he used as a bed in his doings with his Rose-Mary, and he continued to cuddle her against his chest like an infant. From where Saidi was standing while listening to what his boss was telling him about his new responsibilities, he could not help seeing the pool of blood on the seat of the couch and the shreds of the woman's slip and panties just next to it! The office itself was stinking to the skies from the unholy mixture of strong perfumes and deodorants and the odor of sweat from the couple's wrestling match mingled with the smell of sex secretions. And right there in front of him his workplace superior, completely without shame, was cuddling that young woman who was almost naked and kissing her all over her body as if he was possessed and didn't know what he was doing! Saidi son of Jabiri did not know where to run to and escape from the filth of that accursed bastard! And yet his boss was still going on, giving him more instructions: "Now go with this young woman. The driver will take you to her place so that you know where she lives. Then go home. Tomorrow morning, even though it is Sunday, come to work first thing in the morning.

"Take with you this key of my office so that you can come directly in here and clean up everything, you personally, and alone. Clean this couch. The blots you see are nothing but blood and will wash away completely. And you know where to find blot removers for cleaning such seat-covers. Then remove and throw away all rubbish from this office so that everything in here is all clean. On Monday I want to find this office as clean as usual. I think there is no need for me to tell you

I don't want anybody else to know my business with this young woman except you and you alone, today or any other day."

After that he told the young woman to get up and escorted her to the door. The young woman walked while trying her best to hold together the button-less open front of her dress so as to cover her nakedness. There was nothing Saidi could do but follow behind the couple. Outside the door his boss handed over to him his new charge: "The Head Messenger will escort you to your place. And then don't forget! Everything will go as I told you." Executive Chairman Nzoka then went back to his office to wait for his driver to come back from that trip and take him home to his wife Bea and his children.

Saidi did not move from where he stood by the door. When the young woman realized her escort wasn't moving she too stopped dead in her tracks. And then, for the first time, she realized that her shredded dress she was trying her best to hold together in front had a big patch of blood in the seat of her behind! She therefore quickly made for the wall and leaned her back against it to hide the patch of the blood of her virginity, and bent down her head with shame at being seen in such a situation by a messenger, as if saying to herself, "This messenger can really disgrace me, if he decides to tell!"

While Rose-Mary was agonizing over her situation, Saidi turned around and went back to his boss in the office. On seeing him come to the office again, Nzoka shouted at him like a sultan upbraiding his slave: "You are still here! You didn't hear my instructions! What else do you want?"

"Executive Chairman Nzoka, I want you to listen very carefully to what I want to tell you. I am here to work for the corporation. Even if you are the one who brought me here, for me I am here to work for the corporation. Give me work for the corporation, whatever it may be, and at whatever time, I will do the work without saying a word. I am willing and ready to do for you and for any other superior of mine even your personal errands, provided it is the kind of work which a superior can reasonably ask those under him to help him with so that he can be free to attend to more important official duties. That is my duty. But you should never again dare to involve me in your abominable filth! Never again! You can fire me, or do whatever you like. But understand very well that I will never, under any circumstance, let you make me part your filth!" With that Ndugu Head Messenger Saidi son of Jabiri left his boss in his office to deal with his own abominations and got on his way home to his Chiku and his children.

Executive Chairman Nzoka Mwanakulanga could simply not believe it: "A messenger! A nobody of a messenger!! We shall see!"

Ndugu Executive Chairman Nzoka had no choice but to personally escort to her place his young woman in her rags with a bloody seat. But to Ndugu Saidi that was the end of his rank of Head Messenger. And the only thing which saved him from being fired outright was the fact that his Executive Chairman knew all too well that his employee, even though a mere messenger, had come from *Ikulu*, where, like him, he had been working for Mwalimu Nyerere himself. But even then he swore to make him pay: "Let's see where his messenger's lot will get him. He will die in poverty with his ridiculous pride!"

Ndugu Executive Chairman Nzoka's Rose-Mary was staying at Lady Twining Hostel, or Maria Nyerere Hostel, to call it by its new name, and when her Chairman escorted her and found out his beauty was staying at the hostel he decided that was not a place for a young woman like her: "A woman like you shouldn't stay in a such a zoo," he told her. "Every trash of so-called men comes and goes as he pleases in this hostel! No self-respecting man can let his girlfriend stay in a place like this."

The place fit for Rose-Mary to stay was found in Mtoni, a big six-room house. The entire house was rented for her and furnished with sofas and couches and refrigerators and an electric cooker and a gas cooker and all kinds of household accessories a girlfriend of Mzee deserved. A taxi was hired on monthly basis to take her to and from work and wherever she wanted to go, with Mzee footing the bill. I addition, owners of prestigious women clothes and cosmetics shops in the city were instructed to give that young woman whatever she desired in their shops, and bill Mzee. At work Rose-Mary was an ordinary clerk, and at once arrangements were made and completed for sending her for further training at a famous secretarial college in Nairobi. And a few months after that the young half-Mmasai half-Mchaga woman was taken on a shopping spree in preparation for going to her studies in Nairobi, where Mzee would be paying her regular official visits.

On the day Rose-Mary was to fly to Nairobi Executive Chairman Nzoka was too tied up with work. In the morning he had a meeting with President Nyerere in *Ikulu*. And immediately after that he came back to his office to chair the meeting of the Board of Directors of his Corporation, which that day had a long agenda and lasted until nine o'clock at night, by which time Rose-Mary's flight had since long landed in Nairobi and come back to Dar es Salaam for other Nairobi bound passengers. And so Mzee did not escort his beautiful girlfriend to the airport. He left that job to her personal taxi driver, whose taxi for a long time now had been forbidden to carry any other woman in the city or any other passenger at all except Rose-Mary alone.

Ndugu Executive Chairman Nzoka did not arrive back home until ten o'clock at night, all exhausted. He entered his huge mansion in White-town with nothing on his mind but to take a shower at once, and then to eat his wife Bea's great meal of *ugali* of husked corn with a bit of meat and greens deliciously seasoned with peanut milk *à la* Kisukuma, and then his cold bottle of beer, and then sweet sleep.

"That is the great thing with marrying a woman from your place of origin. Your wife knows how to prepare for you your favorite dishes and how to serve you as a woman should serve her husband," Nzoka silently congratulated himself for having a wife like Bea, even though he had never taken his wife who was so good to him to the shops of the Indians in the city so that she too could take whatever she liked there, not even once since they were married.

What welcomed him home this time however was not the pleasure of being treated to a master's traditional due service by a wife from his own ethnicity but his Rose-Mary. His beautiful girlfriend, instead of being in Nairobi, was right there in his living room, comfortably seated as if she was born in the house! And, right there beside her, her suitcases and bags, everything her Mzee bought her!

The wonder of wonders was that the father of that household, instead of asking the young woman what she was doing there instead of being in Nairobi, passed her by as if he hadn't seen her and went to assail with questions his wife, whom he found miserably withdrawn to the kitchen, surrounded by her children.

Rose-Mary arrived there at about six in the evening, by taxi. She knocked at the door and Bea herself opened the door for her and welcomed her into the house. After they exchanged greetings, the visitor asked Bea just one question: "Is this the residence of Executive Chairman Nzoka Mwanakulanga?" Bea answered yes. And, without adding another word, the visitor went to the taxi she came with and began taking out of the car her luggage and bringing it into the house with the help of the taxi driver. As soon as that was done, the taxi left and the young woman took a seat on a couch in the living room and made herself at home. And so Bea too had now to ask her questions, tactfully, since she was a visitor in her home: "How is it? Are you paying us a visit?"

"I am Executive Chairman Nzoka's guest."

"Indeed! What is your name, if I may ask?... Where are you from? Should I telephone and inform him?"

"There is no need. He himself will tell you everything when he comes home."

"Indeed! Very well. I am his wife. My name is Bea. And these are our children. And what is your name, my dear? And what is the nature of your visit to us?"

Rose-Mary kept quiet.

"Yes, please!" Bea pretended to take up something her visitor had said, to reminding her that she was waiting for an answer. She got none.

With that the Msukuma woman understood that her visitor wasn't good news. She therefore decided to go back to her usual household chores and wait for the father of the household to tell her what was going on. And on coming back that head of her family, instead of telling her what that was all about and explaining himself, he straight away came to shout at her with a barrage of questions! "What is this in the house? Who is that woman in the living room?"

"Baba[47] Mayala, I beg you please! Spare me and my children. Don't kill us for no reason! Even if you have decided to throw us out of your home, allow us to leave with our lives!"

Bea was not in the habit of answering back her husband, no matter how much he had annoyed her. She usually would simply say nothing to him, no matter how much he had wronged her. But what was happening there that day wasn't usual. All the same, once she voiced her pent-up anger, because it wasn't her habit to quarrel, she could find nothing to say which would serve any purpose and fell silent and just sobbed with tears streaming from her eyes. That was when her husband realized he had completely lost it. "Mama Mayala, don't cry now! All I want to know is how this woman came here," he quickly changed his words.

"Why don't you go and ask her instead of coming to shout at me? What have I done wrong to you? If she is not your visitor, telephone the police to come and take her away! Or am I the one who was supposed to call them? Since when have I ever interfered with your goings-on with your women? Do you perhaps think I don't know those doings of yours? Do you imagine it gives me pleasure to hear everywhere I go people laughing at me for being a woman who shares her husband with the women of the entire Dar es Salaam! But have you ever heard me ask you a single question about those women of yours, even once?"

Now Bea was pouring out all her grievances pent up in her since nobody knows when. "When did you hear me ask you where you disappear to everyday after work instead of coming home to your children like other fathers do? When did you hear me asking you why you come back to your own home in the dead of the night daily, to the extent that your own children hardly know how you look like and you never know whether they went to bed well or sick, not even for a single day? When did I ever ask you any of that!..." In the end she couldn't go on any longer and just sobbed, joined in by her children, who too began crying when they saw their mother weeping, with the youngest hollering really loud.

The father of the family felt he had to do what he should have done as soon as he entered the house, confront the young woman herself in the living room, and retraced his steps back to her, sweating.

"Rose-Mary, what do you think you are doing! Is this your Nairobi?"

"You never asked me whether I wanted to go to Nairobi or not. Had you asked me, I would have told you not to waste your time, right from the beginning," Rose-Mary answered him, calm and unconcernedly as if she had no idea what was the matter with her dear Executive Chairman to sweat that way in the middle of the night.

"Even then, even if you don't want to go to Nairobi, what are you doing here then?"

"Ah! You really don't know? I am sorry; I didn't know you needed to be told. I am pregnant, for three months. And when my father finds out he will come to kill me. And so I have come here to you, the man who made me pregnant, so that when he kills me he would do so while I am with you."

"You young woman, are you crazy or what?"

"No, I am not crazy at all."

"Don't you know that I am a married man with a wife and children? That I have to protect the respect of my family and my work?"

On hearing that, the Masai blood in the Mchaga young woman boiled like that of Morani warriors of her mother's people in battle. She decided not only to end the conversation, but it was as if she had become completely deaf to the nonsense the man was saying!

In her native Kilimanjaro, from the time she was old enough to know right from wrong, Rose-Mary witnessed her father treat her mother in a way she, though still a little child, felt was not right. It was her mother who, all alone, worked like a donkey cutting grass and bringing it home to feed the cows, weeding the banana and coffee farm, tilling the food crops fields, picking coffee beans, in addition to doing, again all alone, all the household chores, which included fetching water from the stream for her father to bathe at home and boiling and warming it for him first before taking it to him to bathe, while all her father did was just giving orders about everything at home and taking all the money from the coffee crop and spending it on *mbege* banana beer as he pleased! And when her mother dared to complain, however little, about his ways he beat her as if she wasn't a human being but some unwanted dog of his! And when she became a bit older and asked her mother why she was allowing her father to treat her that way, her mother told her that obeying and serving her husband is the most important obligation of a woman on earth. And from that day Rose-Mary decided that in that case she would never get married.

But when she became much older and went to secondary school, she had to modify that resolution of hers.

Another thing Rose-Mary became aware of from very early in her childhood was that everybody, their neighbors and relatives as well as people not related to her at all who saw her said she was very beautiful. She also became aware very early on that adult men jokingly called her their fiancée much more often than they did so with the other little girls of her age at home or in the homes of their neighbors or at the nearby primary school she was attending. In no time she realized that those grown up men, some of them as old as her father, were not joking when they said they were prepared to do anything on this earth in order to marry her. And when her breasts stood fully formed on her bosom and she became a real young woman, especially when she entered Standard IX at Tabora Girls Secondary School, many of those men who said they wanted to marry her now swore that they were quite prepared to do for her whatever she liked or give her anything she wanted on this earth if she consented to sleep with them only once in their entire life! And that was when she reached her final resolve, that, in that case, for her the man who would deflower her would have to pay her diamonds! And the man who had deprived her of her virginity was Executive Chairman Nzoka. She had therefore come to the home of Executive Chairman Nzoka to collect her diamonds. And then the man with her diamonds himself was trying to say nobody knows what nonsense!

After trying in vain to make her say something, and appealing to her to be reasonable and allow him to take her back to her house in Mtoni so that they could look for a better way of handling the matter of her pregnancy without even a sign she was hearing anything he was saying, Executive Chairman Nzoka decided that the best thing to do in those circumstances and in the middle of the night like that, was to let the young woman sleep in the house, in the visitors' room, for the night, and then the following morning he would find a way of taking her back to her place.

Ndugu Executive Chairman Nzoka had come back home late and very tired after a long day at work and then found his home in turmoil from the doings of that young woman, and as a consequence went to bed late, and when he finally went to bed stayed awake for a long time before finding sleep. As a result the following morning he woke up late. And as soon as he woke up he had to hurry to the office and be on time for chairing the still ongoing meeting of his Board of Directors which had been adjourned the previous evening. He therefore left for work before solving the problem of removing the young woman from his home. Except his wife Bea, who on her part didn't sleep a wink the whole night because of the thoughts on her mind and the sadness and pain killing her inside, by the time it dawned she had resolved to confront that young woman who wanted to invade her life that way. If they were going to kill each other, so be it, should she dare refuse to leave her home.

The visitors' room of that house inherited from colonial imperialists was like a house of its own, with everything in it, including a toilet and a bathroom. When Rose-Mary came out of the room at about nine in the morning she had taken a bath and put on her make up and beautified herself and dressed in different clothes from those she wore the previous evening and was walking while whistling to herself as if she was in her own house, on her way to some place, without a single one of the pieces of luggage she came with! She found the mistress of the house seated in the living room and tried to pass her by without greeting her or even looking at her, but the woman of the house wouldn't let her.

"Excuse me, dear woman, but I think we need to talk. You haven't told me how you came to my house without me the owner of the house knowing anything about it!"

"You too excuse me very much, dear woman. But, on my part, what I know is that this house belongs to Chairman Nzoka, who knows everything about my coming here. But, just in case he hasn't told you and you want to know, I have come to stay. If he deflowered you, I too was deprived of my virginity by him. If you have children together, I too am carrying his child. And if you don't believe me ask him. So I think I can go now, I have important things to attend to where I am going. What is more, you and I don't need to quarrel, because I don't have anything at all against you." And with those words the visiting woman got out of the house, and in less than a minute the taxi which brought her the previous day came and took her.

Bea was left in her living room with a drooping head and her heart full of bitterness. What the young woman who had just left said pierced her heart like a poison spear, and that was why she couldn't find even a single word to answer her. Fortunately her children were playing outside and her two house helpers as well as the children's nanny were also busy with their chores somewhere else, otherwise they would all have witnessed her humiliation by that woman in her own home. "So that is it! The man to whom I was wedded, the father of our children, is in love with that concubine of his to the extent of telling her our bed secrets! That he didn't find me a virgin, and she was the one she found a virgin! And so she is the one who deserves being the mistress of this home more! And that is what must have happened. Otherwise how can a woman come from somewhere with all her baggage already done and just crash into the home of a man with a wife and children unless the master of that home himself told her to do so! Even if he made her pregnant, so many married men make young women pregnant all the time and yet we have never heard the like of what this girl did in this world!" The pregnancy of their fifth child Bea was carrying was now really big, in its seventh month. Bea prayed aloud: "Lord my God, help me give birth to my child safely, and then I will leave them their home!"

Bea did not say one word more to that girl and neither did she ask her husband about her again.

In those *naizesheni* days the trend was for men who got high ranking jobs to marry another wife, a more modern one than the mother of their children with whom they came from their lean years of the past. In those days, when women education was not yet widespread in the country, the preferred modern wives of *vizito* of our new nation were mostly Wachaga girls from the region where the girlfriend of Executive Chairman Nzoka, Rose-Mary, came from. Most of those educated girls from Mount Kilimanjaro area were also of light complexion and therefore, according to the colonial and slave mentality of black people worshipping the whites still prevalent at the time, were considered beauties worth everything to a man. When Bea said nothing more while the young woman continued to stay in the house, even though Nzoka hadn't seen any sign of her father or any other relative of hers coming there to try and kill her for getting pregnant before she was married or even to simply inquire about her, Ndugu Executive Chairman decided that it wouldn't be a bad thing at all to make his Rose-Mary his modern spouse, and make his fellow big men die of envy in that respect too. Because when it came to education, his Rose-Mary was educated, and if what mattered most was the light complexion of Wachaga girls, the Wachaga wives of his fellow *vizito* he knew who had married so-called modern wives all without exception would have to kneel before his Rose-Mary all the way down and eat the dust of the ground on which she trod! And when he made that decision, without even waiting for them to get married first, he told her she could move all her belongings from her place in Mtoni to the house if she wanted, and began treating her like his second and favorite wife.

Bea realized that indeed that wasn't her home anymore. She therefore told her husband that she wanted to go home to Bukumbi and deliver her child while staying with their parents, a request to which Nzoka consented all too gladly. On leaving for Bukumbi, Bea felt she had to take all her children with her: "This Mchaga woman isn't a person another woman can leave her children with. A woman who can crash into a man's home this way wouldn't hesitate to do anything at all. She could poison my children's food and kill them all so that no other children are left in this home except those she has come to produce." And so Bea left with all her children and went to Bukumbi. She never came back.

From the very beginning Mwalimu Nyerere was a leader who set examples for the others national leaders to follow. And among the many examples Mwalimu Nyerere set for the other leaders of our country was the need for a leader of *wananchi* to live in a house of his own, build by him, the way Mwalimu himself lived in a house he had build with a loan in Msasani. And as soon as Mwalimu moved into his own house in Msasani, so as to follow his example, every leader in the country got busy building a house so that he would live in a house of his own instead of a government or public corporation house. And the residential district where most of our leaders preferred to build their houses at that time was Msasani Peninsula. That was where our leaders of means erected real mansions, much more impressive than those built during the colonial era in Oyster Bay White-town. As a result in no time a new White-town was born on that peninsula bathed in cool ocean breezes where our leaders erected mansions as if competing to outdo each other.

Among the steps taken by the new Projects, Wealth, Savings and National Development Corporation shortly after it was established, as part of safeguarding its workers interests, was to build good corporation houses for all its high ranking employees. As soon as the construction of those corporation houses started, Executive Chairman Nzoka told the construction companies to also build for him his private residential house on his plot on Msasani Peninsula, after he had taken out a token loan of 75,000 shillings from the National Housing Bank. As a result the construction companies building houses for his corporation erected for him free of charge to him on the peninsula a huge spectacular mansion at a cost of more than three million shillings. The construction of his mansion of a sultan took six months to complete, and his corporation then put in its Chairman's house, again free of charge to him, expensive rugs and pieces of furniture and air conditioners and each and everything needed in the house of an important man and a real *kizito* like Ndugu Executive Chairman Nzoka Mwanakulanga. On the 7th of July, Saba Saba[48] day of 1968, that great son of TANU celebrated the holiday commemorating the founding of his party with a lavish party for the inauguration of his mansion in Msasani Peninsula he had just moved into with his *naizesheni* wife, Roe-Mary, who already wore his wedding ring following their marriage at the District Commissioner's office, and who, on her part, had already rewarded him by the birth of a son, to whom the mother gave the name Pendaeli, her Wachaga people's name meaning "For the Love of God". And Ndugu Nzoka continued to make his fellow bigwigs die of envy! All the dignitaries who flocked to his house-opening party from all over the city left singing the praises of his mansion of a sultan and the expensive things of all kinds it was filled with and the dazzling beauty of his *naizesheni* wife and the ease and elegance with which she received and entertained her guests!

Mwalimu Nyerere's other example to fellow leaders in the nation was for the children of peasants, who made up the majority of our leaders, never to forget their villages of origin. Mwalimu Nyerere did not go on vacation abroad to Europe or other international tourist resorts, as many other leaders of our African countries did. Instead, he always vacationed in his native village of Butiama, where he had built another house of his own for the purpose. And there too our other national leaders and dignitaries zealously followed the example Mwalimu had set them and tried to outdo each other in showing how proud they were of their native villages by erecting there all sorts of expensive houses.

When Bea returned to Bukumbi she did not stay with her parents, who were living in the same neighborhood with the parents of her husband. According to Sukuma customs, she had to live with the parents of her husband, in the home of his husband's father and her father-in-law, Mzee Kulanga, and his grandfather and her grandfather-in-law, Mzee Nzokayape, both of whom were still living, until she delivered the child of their son, and then she would decide what to do next. When she gave birth to her child, before she had time to decide what to do next, her husband went on an official trip to Mwanza. The real purpose of his trip however was to go home to his native Bukumbi and see how his newborn baby and the mother of his child were doing, and to counsel with his wife Bea in the presence of their parents of both sides about their marriage. And he went to Bukumbi well prepared like the real man he was! There were presents for the mother of the newborn, two suitcases of new clothes and shoes and many other presents, and presents for her newborn, two other suitcases full of presents, in addition to lots and lots of presents for his parents and the parents of his wife and all their relatives of both sides, from adults to children! And before he left to go back to Dar es Salaam the counsel of their marriage had taken place and a conclusion reached. His parents as well the parents of his wife Bea all agreed that his decision to marry a second wife was not sufficient reason for them to divorce, if it was indeed true that Nzoka still loved his first and senior wife, to whom he was wedded in church, Bea, and if it was equally true that Bea had no other quarrel with her husband besides the matter of his marrying a second wife. On the question that Nzoka was said to have many other women outside his marriage, their parents of both sides as well as all their other relatives, male and female, who had been asked to participate in the counsel were unanimously of the opinion that such matters could not be discussed by a married couple before their parents, since a man going with other women outside his marriage, if he doesn't bring those women home and they don't make him neglect providing well for his household, cannot be grounds for a quarrel between him and his wife or wives at home. What wasn't quite right was the way Nzoka married his second wife. But even then it wasn't Nzoka's fault but the fault of that second wife of his, who had decided to crash into another woman's home that way instead of waiting until she was married to their shared husband first so that she could come to the man's home the way people's daughters are supposed to go to their husbands' homes when they get married. "Who knows, may be that is their way of doing things in her Wachaga people's land!" their elders reconciled them. The conclusions of that counsel was that Bea was a wife who should go back to her home and live in peace with her husband, and may God bless them with more children, and may they continue to raise all their children well. How Bea was to live with her husband's other wife was a new responsibility facing their husband Nzoka, who had to learn how to handle it well so that his two wives would love each other and he would have a peaceful household.

Nzoka's parents as well as the parents of Bea were all Christians and both their marriages monogamous, nevertheless, that was their consensus and their counsel to Bea and her husband.

Fortunately for Bea going back to her husband did not mean going back to Dar es Salaam to live in the same house with the woman who had invaded her life as if hounded by nobody knows what demon! As soon as the Projects, Wealth, Savings and National Development Corporation was established it opened branches in several regions of the country, the biggest of which was in Mwanza. And when the construction of the residential houses for high ranking officers of the corporation started in Dar es Salaam, the same was done in Mwanza. And Executive Chairman Nzoka made arrangements with the construction companies hired by his corporation to build for him in Kirumba district of Mwanza two houses, a residential house under the name of his first child, his son Mayala, and a commercial building with space for a shop, a bar, and a large dance hall at the back, that one under the name of his second born, also a boy, who had been given the name of the father of his wife Bea, his father-in-law Mabula. And among the special presents he had given his wife Bea for the birth of their fifth child were the keys of those two new houses, the property of her children. As his first wife, Bea was free to choose where she wanted to live, except her husband Nzoka was of the opinion that it would be a good thing for them too to have a second home in Mwanza, Sukumaland, their place of origin, like Mwalimu who had another home in his native Butiama in Zanakiland. Who knows what Providence has in store for us! You may have a job today and be jobless tomorrow. It is prudent for a man to have a place of refuge in his area of origin, should things go wrong for him. "Even when everything is still going well for you, it is commendable for a man to have a place to stay when you are vacationing home where you came from, like Mwalimu Nyerere who has a house in which he stays when vacationing in his native Butiama," Ndugu Nzoka shared his thoughts with his wife in the presence of their parents and other elders. Bea saw all too clearly the cunning way in which her husband wanted to divorce her. Nevertheless and without any hesitation she chose to live in Mwanza. "Why should I knowingly choose to live in humiliation? Over here in Mwanza, in my own home, I will be the master. And if indeed he opens for me a shop and a bar and a restaurant in that house in Mwanza, I will never want anything from anybody in this world in my entire life! I will live happily and comfortably and bring up and educate my children very well indeed, while doing whatever I like as I choose! Have I lost my mind to drag myself back to Dar es Salaam and let that Mchaga prostitute fart into my mouth and feed me on leftovers as if I am not a woman like her?" Bea made up her mind.

From there on Executive Chairman Nzoka became the husband of two wives and with two homes, one on the Coast, in Dar es Salaam, in the new White-town of Msasani Peninsula, and the other one Upcountry, in Mwanza, in his native Sukumaland, *kizito* with solid bases on the Coast and Upcountry.

"How can *mwanachi* and *mzalendo* be more Tanzanian than that? I call home the whole of Tanzania, from the Coast to Upcountry!" he bragged to his fellow leaders and bigwigs.

17

*T*he year 1970 ushered into Tanzania the second phase of the country's *ujamaa* development the Arusha Declaration had launched, the TANU Directive phase whose objective was to entrust the economy and security of the nation into the hands of the masses of *wananchi*.

That year *wananchi* of Tanzania had encountered really frightening news. On their borders, in the neighboring country of Uganda, the President of the country, Milton Obote, had been overthrown in a military coup by his armed forces, and Idi Amin, a brutal murderer, fascist and terrible monster, had taken over the Government of the country. It became clear to our leaders in the Party and the Government that the greatest enemy of the people's interests and well-being, especially in young countries like our African ones, was not the enemies from outside our borders. The greatest enemy of Tanzania with its policies of *ujamaa* with self-reliance was not the capitalists and imperialists of the world, and neither was it the accursed Boers with their racist oppression of the black people of South Africa and Rhodesia, nor the doomed dying-age Portuguese colonial masters of Angola and neighboring Mozambique and all the other decaying colonialists wherever they are still clinging onto our Continent of Africa. Our greatest enemy, and the one most difficult to guard against, was the internal one: individuals greedy for power and the amassing of wealth. As the Swahili people say, what bites you is in your clothes. The only way to really protect the independence of the nation and the country's economy against brigands like the Monster

Idi Amin is to place the security of the nation in the hands of *wananchi* themselves, under their own army, their *Mgambo*[49] Army.

Wananchi were informed of that and responded with determination to the call to be the first line of defense for their country's independence, security and economy. Because the *Mgambo* army was an army of the masses of peasants and workers of Tanzania, it had to involve their leaders as well. And Executive Chairman Nzoka Mwanakulanga became the very first leader in the nation to volunteer for the *Mgambo* army training. And he didn't join the *Mgambo* training only for show, so as to have his photograph in the newspapers and to be seen in the heavy cotton khaki uniform of the *Mgambo* soldiers, as many of his fellow leaders would compete to do later, just as the Christians among them were competing to appear at mass at St. Peters Church in the city at the time Mwalimu Nyerere went to pray on Sunday morning so that Mwalimu could see what God-fearing leaders they were. Nzoka Mwanakulanga joined the *Mgambo* training so as to become a real *Mgambo* soldier, with the result that when he finished his training he was selected to become a Commander in charge of the training of new *wananchi* recruits. And the first civilian Commander of the *Mgambo* Army, Ndugu Executive Chairman Nzoka, likewise excelled by his ardor and skill at training *Mgambo* recruits, as if he was a real military commander! Nobody who saw him on Jangwani grounds or Chikubu premises in Ubungo or the sports grounds of the University of Dar es Salaam conducting his *mchaka mchaka*[50] troops by a song in his native Kisukuma mixed with a bit of Swahili, a whistle on the mouth, could have guessed he was an important national leader with an office job! Physically too, Executive Chairman Nzoka looked different from many of his fellow big shots, who on getting their high ranking jobs with their abundant fringe benefits began eating like pigs and became fat and with huge bellies like a woman expecting twins! For him among the things which impressed him most during his study trips abroad were the programs for keeping the human body fit and in good health. He therefore ate and drunk in moderation and exercised regularly so as to keep his body in good shape. And on his *Mgambo* duty he looked a real civilian-soldier! It was impossible to guess he was the greatest *naizesheni* in the country by looking at the energetic young man he was!

When the *Mgambo* campaign flared on until it reached all offices and factories and other places of work and spread to all the regions of the country, all the way to the villages, Mwalimu Nyerere and his fellow Party and Government leaders were satisfied the *Mgambo* army of Tanzania was now fully formed. What remained in strengthening the security of the nation was to make the armed forces of the country, the Tanzania *Wananchi* Army, part and parcel of that *Mgambo* army as well as its fortress. So as to marry the *Mgambo* army of the masses of Tanzania with their country's armed forces, two important steps were taken. First, branches of the party of *wananchi* of Tanzania, TANU, were opened in the armed forces, under the leadership of the commanding officers of the Army's different sections. Secondly, it was decided that civilian leaders who were really politically mature and trusted *wazalendo* should join the Tanzania *Wananchi* Army by taking military courses and becoming commissioned officers of the Army and part of its leadership. Ndugu Executive Chairman Nzoka, the first civilian Commander of *Mgambo* Army, was in the very first intake of civilian leaders selected to go to the Army Leadership Academy in Monduli. And while in Monduli Ndugu Executive Chairman Nzoka proved that indeed he was a solid leader and a real civilian-soldier. As a result when his group graduated he was commissioned as a full Lieutenant instead of Second Lieutenant, the intended rank for the course.

Mwalimu Nyerere was greatly pleased by the success his assistant-leader of so many years. As a result as soon as he finished his military course, instead of going back to his office like his colleagues with whom he graduated from Monduli, who all went back to their posts and continued with their former jobs as usual and became commissioned army officers only in name, Mwalimu sent him for further military training in Great Britain and Canada, to take courses in Espionage and Army Security. And when he graduated from his studies abroad and retuned home he was immediately promoted and made Major, and in no time he had become Colonel. And he was not a Colonel in name only, but one with a really important military job: he became the ears and eyes of Mwalimu Nyerere and the Party and the Government in the army, whose job was to make sure that, God willing, Tanzania would be spared what befell *wananchi* of Uganda and burdened them with the untold sufferings of the rule of the Monster Idi Amin. Ndugu Nzoka therefore became a leader wearing two hats, both carrying heavy responsibilities, the military one and that of his old post, since he also continued heading that very important corporation of the Tanzanian public.

Our national policy, especially since the Arusha Declaration, is that of independence with self-reliance. Our economy therefore depends first and foremost on the peasants and workers, especially the low income workers, and the rest of the toiling masses, who are the Tanzanian public. In spite of that, it is also true that the greater part of our national wealth remains in the hands of a few businessmen, most of whom are of foreign origin, especially the Indians. And even though almost all those foreign businessmen are Tanzanians citizens, since the inauguration of the Arusha Declaration many of them feared the possible hatred and envy of the poor masses of the country against them on account of their wealth. And right from the start they realized that their most effective protection was in sharing their wealth with the new leaders of the country. And because of that Ndugu Executive Chairman Nzoka, from the day he was appointed by Mwalimu Nyerere to head that important public corporation under which fell almost every kind of business in the country, became a very wealthy leader indeed. Following the take over of Uganda by the Monster Amin in 1970, the fear of those Tanzanian businessmen of foreign origin turned into panic. There was nobody on earth who hated the Monster Amin right from the beginning more than the people of Tanzania, because, besides his brutal massacring of thousands upon thousands of *wananchi* of Uganda, his criminal rule started off with his provocation and unacceptable annoyance of Tanzania. But, in spite of that, when that accursed monster decided to confiscate the property of the citizens of Uganda of Indian origin, after he had illegally taken away from them their citizenship and expelled them from the country, the ordinary people of Tanzania throughout the country applauded his action! Indian-Tanzanians panicked and were really terrified! They realized that, unless they took appropriate steps, what had befallen their relatives in Uganda could happen to them too. The really wealthy ones among them therefore did everything they could to take out of the country all their money and to look for ways of safeguarding their properties they couldn't take out by entering into business partnership with national leaders capable of helping them and willing to do so. And from that moment Ndugu Executive Chairman Nzoka became a real tycoon of international stature.

From the time he was appointed head of that public corporation in 1967, Chairman Nzoka had not been able to go on vacation even in a single year. His work at his corporation, his *Mgambo* duties, his army responsibilities, his role in the meetings of the Board of Director of numerous other public corporations associated with his corporation in whose administration, by special appointment by President Nyerere, he was involved on account of his leadership expertise, had left him no time for taking a vacation. When in 1979 he could finally take some vacation he had accumulated annual leave of more than ten years. His corporation had just received an invitation from the Government of West Germany to send one of its managers to the country to attend a special nine months international course on World Markets and Merchandizing Strategies. Executive Chairman Nzoka decided to use his accumulated days of annual leave by taking that course in Germany and refreshing his mind, lest he became a rusty leader.

Rose-Mary was now a woman who had already given birth to several children. When she came to that home she found the other wife of their husband, Bea, already with four children and pregnant with a fifth one, to whom she gave birth before she had delivered the child of her loss of virginity. Before she got married she was resolved never to have more than one child, since giving birth to many children ages a woman fast. But on finding the other wife of that home already with such a huge advantage over her she decided to open fully wide her womb until the very last child her Creator put in there was out, especially since it was already the practice of the master of that home that a woman bearing him a child meant the mother having a new house built for her, in the name of her newborn, and in a location of her choice! And when her husband was setting out for his trip to Germany his Rose-Mary had already born him six children.

So now Rose-Mary, even though still a beautiful and fashionable woman who took good care of herself, to a womanizer for ever chasing after new conquests like Nzoka had become just an ordinary woman. Her breasts, which used to stand erect on her bosom like spears and to burn the body of a man like hot cooking stones, after suckling six children now needed tightly wrapping up in a bra before her dress could sit well on her bosom. Her husband's kisses which had deprived her of her virginity weren't hers anymore; they were for the countless young ravishing beauties who were taking turns to entertain that master of theirs on the couches of his office and in tourist hotel rooms all over the country. In short, her turn to be the stay-at-home wife like Bea was when she came into that home of their husband had arrived. Fortunately that did not worry or trouble Rose-Mary at all. She was the one sitting on the diamond mine. All the other women of that man, including his first wife, who wed the man in church, were women who depended on charity and alms, who existed on the leftovers of the one and only Rose-Mary, herself. So, why should she worry! Only the woman who would dare try to uproot her from there was the one who needed to come very well prepared indeed! At any rate that would never happen because, before it happened, the man who shit the diamonds they were fighting over would no longer be in this world. She would kill him. By whatever means it took. She was therefore completely indifferent when her husband, after returning from Germany at the beginning of 1980, within a short while brought into the country a European woman, who had already born him a son, and for whom he had already completed building a house on Kigamboni beach in the city.

That third wife of his was a German professor he met at the course he took in her country. Dr. Helene Peters, as she was called, a woman of thirty-six years of age, was one of the Economics specialists from a number of German universities who presented papers at the international seminar he was attending. That was how they met. To Chairman Nzoka, that woman was just another woman to have sex with. But the white woman on her part believed and treasured every word that expert seducer of women told her, every sweet word he whispered into one of her ears and into the other one, every kiss he implanted here and there and everywhere on her! As a result when she gave herself completely to him and their love affair was in full swing, the woman was already deadly in love with Ndugu Nzoka, and each time they made love her body told her she had never known the intoxicating ecstasy of sex until the day his African lover first made love to her. She was aware that he was a married man and a passer-by from a far off country, but all the same her love for him made her desire to have a child by him, especially since she had reached the age when women who don't get married early begin to give up on ever finding a man to marry them and decide to have a child by a man they chanced to like who comes along, lest they became too old to have children while still waiting to get married first before having children. "Should he leave me with a child, it would be his greatest present to me. It would be the fruit of our love which would for ever remind me, for as long as I remain in this world, of the wonders of our love," the female professor resolved. And indeed she became pregnant. And when she informed him she was expecting a baby, her African lover answered, very calmly as if it was something he already knew and had been thinking about it for a long time: "Our love has been blessed by the Almighty God. If you had no objection to being married to a man with two wives already, I would marry you right away."

The German woman could not believe her ears! She was an educated woman who knew that there are countries in the world where it is not illegal to marry more than one wife and that Tanzania, where her lover came from, was one of them. There was therefore nothing more for her to say except to agree with her lover, "Indeed God has blessed our love!" That was how that white woman became the third wife of Ndugu Executive Chairman Nzoka and made that leader of our people come back home laughing to himself all the way to the skies: "This one will simply finish them off! Make them know that there are dignitaries and dignitaries, men and men! Who among them has an international catch like her for a wife? And she is not just some white woman and nothing else. She is a very highly educated woman and a renowned specialist, a Professor. She has been married by a Msukuma boy who didn't go beyond Standard X," he said to himself, thinking of how his fellow dignitaries would die of envy and salivating on account of his international trophy with white skin. And his international trophy once in Tanzania didn't just rest on the laurels of her husband's fame. She immediately occupied a very important post: the very first Director of the newly created Department of External Trade in her husband's corporation, the Projects, Wealth, Savings and National Development Corporation of Tanzania. And so the social standing of Executive Chairman Colonel Nzoka Mwanakulanga was enhanced beyond that of any of his peers, by their reckoning.

And those who thought they had seen the end of him didn't know Ndugu Nzoka. Before even a year had gone by since he brought his European wife into the country, one of his Indian business partners with shops and all kinds of other businesses all over the country decided to further cement their business ties by giving him his daughter in marriage. The Indian tycoon was a devout Moslem and before Ndugu Nzoka could marry his daughter he had to convert to Islam first. And for Ndugu Nzoka, even though he was a Christian, and the son and grandson of Christians, doing so was a very small matter indeed: "All these foreign religions to us the Africans are religions of criminal invaders who had nothing but contempt for a black person. Otherwise they are in no way better than the traditional religions of our people, which some of us don't even know anything about, unless it is to consider them the religions of savages. What harm can having one more or less of such religions do? The important thing is that I will marry an Indian treasure?" Ndugu Nzoka therefore became a Moslem, with the name of Muhamedi, and was duly wed to his new bride. Ndugu Executive Chairman Colonel Nzoka decided to let his Indian wife live among her fellow Indians in Upanga, the center of residential India-town of the city of Dar es Salaam, and bought for her a beautiful two-story house in Upanga East near the home of her parents, his partners in the world of great people. And his fellow dignitaries had to surrender and admit defeat: "This man is no longer one of us! Prosperity of this kind can't be normal! It must be his Wasukuma people's magic at work!"

18

*I*n spite of Executive Chairman Colonel Nzoka being the envy of his fellow big shots for having been blessed by the Almighty God beyond measure, for being the *kizito* of *vizito* and the man among men, a man with wives from the four corners of the world, a man every beautiful woman in the entire city of Dar es Salam was dying for, there was one woman in the city who held his heart captive. His incomparable woman was an uneducated woman in *Uswahilini* of Magomeni, Mama Ntwara. Nzoka knew the mother of that woman, Grandma Ntwara, almost from the first day he arrived in Dar es Salaam, through his fellow employee at TANU Party Headquarters, Saidi, who received him in the city and stayed with him for a long time at his home in Kariakoo, next door to the home of that adoptive mother of Ndugu Saidi. And when in 1967 Grandma Ntwara, in her effort to be self-reliant in independent Tanzania of *Ujamaa*, opened a beer store for her daughter at her home in Magomeni, Nzoka was among the very first customers of the store, which became a hit right away on account of that daughter of hers, Mama Ntwara. And Ndugu Nzoka was also among the very first of our potentates to make love to that Mmakonde woman, over whom men who were real *vizito* fought as soon as she arrived in the city. Because that was the year he was appointed to head the greatest of the nation's public corporations, Nzoka entered that battle over the love of the Mmakonde woman with a decisive advantage over all his competitors. As it happened, the Mmakonde woman too proved an expert at distinguishing real important men from those pretending to be so and chose Chairman Nzoka among her many clients, all big shots, who wanted her. And from there on, that woman, the fame of whose cultural skills in bed had spread throughout Dar es Salaam, became the exclusive private domain of Chairman Nzoka. All other men, however important and powerful, to that woman who made men crazy with her rumored wonders in bed and the shape of her body and the way she moved became just clients of her store to whom she only smiled and served beer and roast meat and stewed goat-head meat and cow-hoof soup. And being singled out by that woman as her favorite and only man pleased Nzoka so much and he became so fond of her that he built her a house before he had given such a big present to a single one of his wives. And after building her that residential house, which the woman decided to rent to tenants, he built her a Bar and Lodging at K's Corner in Mwananyamala, which was the first bar of that kind in the whole of Dar es Salaam and earned his beloved woman lots of money. And as days went by and their love ripened and took real hold of them, he built her two more lodging houses, one in her Magomeni neighborhood and another one in Kinondoni, as his way of thanking her for the great time he was having with her. And if in this world there was a woman who really knew how to show her love for a man, it was that Mmakonde woman. It is said that even the hottest women cool off a bit as they age, but the incomparable woman of Ndugu Executive Chairman Colonel Nzoka was another matter altogether. Year in and year out, as time went by so did that Mmakonde woman's bed-pleasure skills which drove men crazy continue to grow! And Chairman Nzoka too continued to thank her for that by heaping all sorts of presents on her!

By 1985 Mama Ntwara had become a very wealthy woman whose properties included countless bars and lodgings and residential houses for renting. Her two children she came with from Mtwara were both now grown up. Both of them had been educated by Chairman Nzoka, their mother's Mzee. The elder, the boy, whose name was Hasani, had stopped schooling at the end of Form IV, and then stayed home to help her mother with running her businesses. He was now an adult man married and living with his wife and children in his own home in their Magomeni neighborhood. He was the manager of all his mother's businesses and properties as well as those of his grandmother, the late Grandma Ntwara. His younger sister, whose name was Zainabu, had just finished Form VI at Jangwani Girls Secondary School in the city and passed her examination with flying colors, and had been admitted to the University of Dar es Salaam, to study Engineering, and her mother and her mother's Mzee who educated her were really pleased with her for that. Even though now the education of girls had much improved and the number of female students at the university had increased considerably, still only very few of them qualified for taking degrees in Engineering. A big festivity was therefore held for her by her mother and their Mzee at her mother's place in Magomeni to celebrate her success.

Zainabu was a girl who had been raised by a mother and grandmother who knew all about men. She had therefore been warned since very early in her life to beware of men and to keep herself out of danger in her relationship with them. As a result she had protected herself by having nothing at all to do with men. And indeed she grew up and reached puberty and continued with her schooling until she finished Form IV still safe and sound, with no relationship of any kind with any man, without even a boy with whom she exchanged childish love letters or a boyfriend with who to sneak out and go to cinema now and then, because she had been very well taught by her mother how to put off any boy who wanted to be too familiar with her. It was when she went to Form V and had to stay in a dormitory at Jagwani Girls Secondary School, as was required by the school regulations at the time, that she became acquainted for the first time with that most important matter in the lives of all girls, of loving and being loved by men. However she embarked on it in a rather different way from that of most girls of her age. She was not attracted to the countless young men who said they loved her, and not only those who were just after having a good time with her, but even those who were seriously courting her and wanted to marry her. Right from the beginning Zainabu chose to make love with adult men only, men as old as her father, if not older. And among all those sugar daddies of hers she made love with, she chose to stick to her mother's Mzee, Executive Chairman Nzoka, who put her through school as if she were his own daughter, while knowing fully well and since she was a little child that the Mzee was not an ordinary friend of her mother but a great lover of hers! As to the Mzee himself, to Ndugu Executive Chairman Colonel Nzoka being loved by the mother and her daughter that way was further evidence that he was a man among men, *kizito* of *vizito*, a master among masters. "As long as they are not my blood relatives," he soothed his conscience. So by the time she completed Form VI at Jangwani the daughter of Mama Ntwara had become one of Chairman Nzoka's numerous concubines. And the party he threw to celebrate her admission to the University of Dar es Salaam was on one side, for her as his child, the daughter of his concubine, and on the other side, for his spring chicken. And when in July of 1985 Zainabu moved into Hall III, the dormitory for female students at the University of Dar es Salaam, she went there in style, intent on silencing all the young women who had ever attended the university since its inauguration who dared brag of a special status. Among the luggage she went with at the start of her studies at the university was a new car, a Range Rover, a present from her Mzee!

When Mama Ntwara at her home in Mgomeni got the information and the whole truth about the relationship between that lover of hers and her daughter was confirmed, she swore in her native Kimakonde she could not live on the same earth with that accursed bastard of a man. "This dog with its tail must be removed from this earth. And must depart from the earth without that tail of his, so that the whole world would know he died because of the abominations of his tail!" Mama Ntwara concluded her Kimakonde oath dooming her great lover.

Chairman Nzoka had just bought Mama Ntwara too an automobile, a pickup truck, Toyota 4-Wheel-Drive Double-Cabin, with windows so dark a person on the outside couldn't see inside, even though she had another pickup, also still new. Ever since the Government decided that, even though the importation of cars had been banned, *wananchi* could import such load-carrying vehicles, because they weren't luxury automobiles but work tools which increase the capacity of *wananchi* to transport goods and agricultural and industrial inputs for the development of our economy, *wananchi* of means imported many such pickup trucks from Japan, especially used ones which had been reconditioned. Executive Chairman Colonel Nzoka too used that opportunity to buy for each and everyone of his wives and concubines those utility trucks, except he ordered only brand-new ones. "It is an unbearable insult to a real man with his dignity to buy for his wife or concubine a reconditioned vehicle, some junk which had bee thrown away into a rubbish dump by other people," he told his fellow big shots who considered those reconditioned vehicles valuable property. And when his incomparable love of *Uswahilini* complained that new pickup trucks had become what every woman in the city had, he bought her that top-of-the-line pickup. Chairman Nzoka's beloved woman of *Uswahilini* Mgomeni had therefore every reason to feel she was a woman among women in the zoo of women of all ages who were entertaining and catering to the pleasure of that *kizito* leader, had her master not wronged her so grievously by making the child from her own womb another concubine of his.

Mama Ntwara decided that the best way to bring that master of theirs into her hands without delay was to pretend she knew nothing and let his tail and its rottenness bring him to her so that she could teach the accursed bastard what a woman like herself was all about and what a daughter meant to her mother!

And indeed before a week passed Ndugu Nzoka informed his Mmakonde love that he was coming to take a rest in her home that day. At the home of that uneducated *Uswahilini* woman was where the famous man took refuge when in need of solace whenever he was overwhelmed with his domestic or work related problems. It was Mama Ntwara alone who was aware that even an important and powerful man like him has days when he needs to rest his head on the breasts of the woman he loves and let her soothe him like a mother who gives a breast to her crying baby to suckle accompanied by a song and the baby is lulled and stops crying. To the rest of his women he was the father of their children or Executive Chairman Nzoka and nothing else. It was only Mama Ntwara who saw him as her lover besides everything else. And then she was a woman of incomparable bed-skills, to the extent that, even though Ndugu Executive Chairman Colonel Nzoka now was no longer a young man, every time they made love he wanted to have it the whole night long!

When he arrived at her home in Magomeni that evening Mama Ntwara received him in her usual way. First he took a warm bath, and then he was served a great meal, from pilaf rice to *ugali* of husked corn flour accompanied with fish from Mwanza where he came from and greens of different kinds really deliciously seasoned with butter and peanut milk like the greens of his grandmother's cuisine in his native Bukumbi. And then he was given a cold beer, something to drink while his mistress was preparing herself for her bedtime cultural show, by bathing, then anointing and perfuming and powdering her body, and then warming and scenting her female parts with an assortment of incenses by bestriding a brazier from which the incense were smoking.

As soon as the smell of incense reached Executive Chairman Nzoka, he hurried up and finished the beer he had been sipping slowly in the sitting room while listening to the lyrics of some heart-rendering love songs of *taarabu*[51] music, another form of entertainment his was treated to only at the home of his Magomeni *Uswahilini* love among all his mistresses.

In the bedroom he found his Mmakonde mistress already in bed and with lights off. Chairman Nzoka too at once took off the piece of *kanga* his mistress had given him to wrap around his nakedness while she was getting ready to welcome him to bed. He remained as naked as he was born and made for the bed, ready to dance with his woman her Makonde people's love-dance. But as he was about to climb into bed his love stopped him; "Wait first. Put on the lights!"

"Ah! You too, Mama Ntwara! You forget your lover is an old man now!" Executive Chairman Nzoka complained, as he went to the wall and switched on the lights. One of the games they played as part of their cultural bed-show was Mama Ntwara always asking him to put on the lights first before coming to bed to make love to her, so that she could see how erect his male member was, claiming that if it was rather limp that was proof he had just slept with his other women and was exhausted, or he didn't love her anymore. And it was taboo for Mama Ntwara to allow a man to enter into her his good for nothing tail if she had to touch and play with it and coax it first before it got erect. And so when Chairman Nzoka put on the lights in the room and turned around so that his mistress could see how deserving he was of being held in her arms in bed, his tail was already as erect as a pole and swollen like an angry cobra and he was wagging it this way and that way for his love to see how strong and fit he still was! But, instead of congratulations from his woman in bed, on turning around he found that mistress of his standing in front of him, upright like a soldier in battle, and holding high up in the air with her two hands a big knife, as long as a sword and double-edged like the spear of Masai warriors, which she at once brought down with all her strength to cut off in one stroke her lover's tail! Fortunately Nzoka spotted the danger in time to jump back and the huge knife missed by a hair amputating and castrating him terribly! Even then there was nowhere for him to run in the bedroom with a closed door. He had jumped back right into the wall behind him and there was no further way of escape for him. Mama Ntwara went for him at the wall, with the steps of a hunting lioness, her double-edged machete up in the air again and flashing in the lights. Ndugu Executive Chairman Nzoka urinated and shit all over himself on the spot. And fortunately that became his saving act. "There is no need to bother killing a dog like you, and go to jail and be hanged because of a male creature who has a tail but in fact is not even a man! What kind of a man shits on himself like he has diarrhea to the point of death for fear of a woman!" And with that decision by Mama Ntwara he was saved. Instead of death by castration he was just thrown out of the house as naked as he was born and dirty all over with the filth of his shit and urine, without his mistress even deigning to throw outside for him his clothes he had taken off ready to enjoy her cultural bed-treat.

Mama Ntwara's neighbors took pity of Executive Chairman Colonel Nzoka out on *Uswahilini* streets in Magomeni at that time of about nine o'clock at night and found him a taxi to take him back home to his Rose-Mary and his children in Msasani Peninsula White-town, dressed in nothing but an old piece of cloth wrapped around his nakedness, a worn-out *kanga* a very old woman was wearing and took off and gave to him in the crowd of *wananchi* of Magomeni who witnessed that free show of the goings-on of the great ones of our society.

Nzoka was disgraced, but it is not easy to fight a powerful man. When he was disgraced that way, he decided that the only way to teach a lesson that accursed savage of a woman was to marry her daughter outright. And indeed Zainabu, Miss Range Rover as she was called by her fellow students on Mlimani,[52] became the fifth wife of her mother's Mzee! And so as to teach that great love of his of so many years an even greater lesson, he made her daughter change religion, renounce Islam and convert to the religion of his birth, Christianity, and had her baptized in his Roman Catholic sect as Mary-Rose, with the names of his great love of yesteryear, his second wife Rose-Mary, in reverse order. And he didn't stop there. After his conversion to Islam so that he could marry his Indian wife, he had gone on a pilgrimage to Mecca with his Moslem wife and he now had the title of Alhaji as well. The Roman Catholic Christian Moslem, Executive Chairman Colonel Alhaji Muhamedi Nzoka Mwanakulanga decided to confound the whole world and to teach everybody a lesson by marrying his fifth wife, Zainabu Mary-Rose, in the Roman Catholic Church, which not only prohibits polygamy but also does not allow divorce, while his wife Bea was alive and still married to him, living in his home of Mwanza! And his marriage was duly celebrated at St. Joseph's Cathedral in the city, with a Great Mass sang in Latin, Swahili and Arabic and officiated by forty priests and concluded by the reading of greetings and blessings for the bride and bridegroom from the Pope of the Catholic Church sent specially for them. Since Ndugu Nzoka was still bound by another holy matrimony to his wife Bea, ordinarily he would have been considered by the Catholic Church as a man living in sin, since he had more than one wife, but, by special dispensation, at the mass of his marriage to his fifth wife he and his bride received Holy Communion, the sign of people with pure souls in the eyes of our Creator! And the reception which followed the mass was attended by the leaders of all the churches in the country, all the great Moslem sheikhs in the city of Dar es Salaam, all important Party and Government leaders and all the diplomats from the foreign embassies in the country! Ordinary dignitaries and leaders had to bribe with lots of money the ushers at the gate to get invitation cards for the reception party! Ndugu Executive Chairman Colonel Alhaji Muhamedi Nzoka Mwanakulanga had indeed earned the right to brag even more: "How can a man be greater than this here on earth!"

Ndugu Nzoka bought a two-storied house for his fifth wife in Sinza, next to the University of Dar es Salaam, so that she could continue with her studies without the inconvenience of driving her car from far away. And Zainabu Mary-Rose in return thanked her Mzee and her mother's Mzee of many years by bearing him a son a few months after their historic wedding. His father decided to give that son of his the warrior name of Imara.[53] He accompanied the naming of his child by giving himself too a new name: "From now on my name is Ndugu *Alhamdulillahi*," he proclaimed, standing upright on the verandah of the second floor of the house of his fifth wife, a grin spreading cross his face, while holding up in the air with his two hands his infant child, both child and father facing east as if he was uttering a Moslem prayer!

And from that day indeed Ndugu Executive Chairman Nzoka wanted to be called Ndugu *Alhamdulillahi* by everybody. Now when a person greeted him he answered that person's greetings with "*Alhamdulillahi!*" Whenever a person asked how he was doing he answered by "*Alhamdulillahi!*" Even when someone greeted him with "Good morning, Mzee!" his answer remained one and the same: "*Alhamdulillahi!*" Finally all over the city he became known by his new name of Ndugu *Alhamdulillahi*, or Ndugu Mzee *Alhamdulillahi*.

19

*N*dugu Executive Chairman Colonel Nzoka had every right to feel *Alhamdulillahi*. By that year of 1985, when he bought his fifth wife, Zainabu Mary-Rose, her home in Sinza, that leader of ours and *kizito* of *vizito* in the country had a total of thirty-two children, twenty-seven of them by his five wives and the remaining five by his concubines.

His European wife, who came to the country already with one child of his, decided to have a second one, and gave birth to a baby girl this time, before going back to her homeland of origin, Germany, to have her tubes tied, since apparently where she came from two children are considered too many. His Indian wife he married in 1980 gave birth from the start in a truly Indian way and by 1985 she had given birth three times, and to twins each time. She had therefore already born him six children. Together with the daughter of his incomparable love Mama Ntwara, Zainabu Mary-Rose, his three younger wives alone had born Ndugu Executive Chairman Nzoka a total of nine children. And his first wife Bea in her home in Mwanza had continued bearing children for him without cease throughout all those years until she had twelve children. Some *Waswahili* were saying that the secret of those children was known by their mother Bea alone. To Executive Chairman Nzoka however that was utter nonsense and all of them were his children like any other children of his, because that great leader of ours, who was the confidant of so many married women, was convinced that since the beginning of time only the mother knows the secret of her child, even when that mother was a wife who had never slept outside her husband's home even once since she was married! God had curtailed the plan of his wife number two, Rose-Mary, by unjustly ending early her child-bearing when she had resolved to have more children than the first wife of their husband and continue besting her even after kicking her out and packing her off all the way to Mwanza. In spite of that she too bore Ndugu Executive Chairman Nzoka those six children. And then outside his five marriages he had five other children, three with an uneducated woman from *Uswahilini* Ilala in the city, one with the wife of a man in Mwanza whose marriage he had ended that way, and one with a girl he made pregnant when she was in Form I at a secondary school in Arusha, the conference-holiday-resort city of the great ones of our country.

By that year of 1985 the country's economy had collapsed completely and a person living in dire poverty, incapable of affording the barest necessities of life, was no longer the lot of the likes of Saidi son of Jabiri and his fellow have-nots only but had become the reality of life even for government or public corporation employees with good jobs who depended solely on their salaries. *Wananchi* who felt they had the necessary qualifications were fleeing the country in search of greener pastures abroad. It was no longer possible even for a manager of a public corporation who depended on his or her salary alone to buy meat for the people of his or her home as often as he or she wanted, or even to give his or her children a breakfast of bread with tea. In the past, in the homes of those black-white men everyday parents had to struggle really hard and coax their children to make them eat the food they were served, their spoilt children wanting their mothers to cook for each one of them whatever he or she happened to desire! Now that was ancient history. Now the mothers of White-town too had become experts at making *yanga* gruel like the Chikus of

Manzese and everywhere in *Uswahilini* of the city. At best the difference between them was that some of those wives of the great ones could still afford to sprinkle a bit of sugar on the unpalatable *yanga* instead of making it with salt.

But Executive Chairman Nzoka lived in a totally different Tanzania from that of his fellow *wananchi*. All his wives and concubines and their children together with all his relatives and in-laws with their relatives, every person Chairman Nzoka considered as having a claim on him, didn't even know what *yanga* was! In fact at his main home, the home of his second wife Rose-Mary in Msasani Peninsula where he lived, the mistress of that home had banned even *ugali* of husked corn, the favorite food of people of means, unless it was made with butter and milk instead of water alone! And often even *ugali* of butter and milk served at her home was made of the flour of ground rice, at a time when rice had become so rare that the children of the have-nots of Tanzania could eat it only in their dreams! And every meal at the homes of the multitude of dependants of that leader of ours, wherever they were, was always served with fish and meat and greens of their choice!

Some years back the Government had nationalized butcheries and the meat industry in the country and put it under public corporations, so that profits from that important business would benefit all *wananchi* instead of only a handful of capitalist fat cats who had been monopolizing the business. The result however proved to be the exact opposite. The price of meat skyrocketed and the public corporation entrusted with running the business all became bankrupt and rotten to the core from corruption and theft, causing the Government and the people of Tanzania a great loss of revenue while rendering despicable service to customers! The Government had no option but to close down or take away the business of almost all those public corporation and the meat industry went back to private business owners. Chairman

Nzoka was among the biggest *bubu*[54] owners of those private butcheries, most of which ended up in the hands of our leaders. That business of his in the city was run by his Wachaga in-laws, the brothers of his wife Rose-Mary, in a partnership with the Arabs and Indians who owned most of the butcheries in the city. Therefore all his dependents could not want meat on any day. By his instructions, each and every one of his countless dependents listed his or her meat needs for a week and, once Mzee approved the list, it became a done deal. And in that meat business Nzoka was a crucial partner, since he was also in the business of bringing cattle from Mwanza and Shinyanga to the cattle auction at Pugu on the outskirts of Dar es Salaam. He had entrusted the business of buying cattle whole-sale to his first wife, Bea, in Mwanza, in collaboration with his own brothers and his brothers-in-law from their native Bukumbi, who now brought to Dar es Salaam every week herds upon herds of cattle from upcountry. Chairman Nzoka with his Mwanza wife and their Wasukuma relatives also had control of another lucrative business of transporting to Dar es Salaam by air fresh fish from Lake Victoria which was in great demand to the multitudes of city-dwellers who hailed from the Lake region. They were also in control of an even more lucrative business of transporting by train to the city dried fish from that lake abounding with fish. At the same time Chairman Nzoka was also entrenched, again silently, in the fish market at Ferry in Dar es Salaam. He was also involved in a big way in chicken farming, both for meat and egg layers, even though there wasn't a single chicken or chick anywhere in the home of any of his wives and concubines or relatives! And then he had deep roots in the business of green vegetables, fruits, tomatoes and onions, sweet potatoes and cassava, and the staples of our people, corn, rice and beans, in the main city markets of Kariakooo, Ilala, Mgomeni and Manzese. Ndugu *Alhamdulillahi* Nzoka therefore had every right to boast that it was prohibited to any person who was related to him in any way anywhere in the country to be in want of any kind of food!

Even though people were living under impossible conditions, everybody had realized the value of education and all parents still wanted to give their children the best education possible. But the reality of life was that the seventh grade of primary school for the masses of Tanzanian parents was all the education they could afford to give their children. A lucky parent whose child succeeded and was selected to go to Form I of a public secondary school thanked God earnestly, especially since educating a child in a paying private secondary school was beyond the wildest dreams of ordinary Tanzanians. But, in that respect too, Executive Chairman Nzoka lived in an altogether different Tanzania. His very first child, his son Mayala, was in that year of 1985 studying Economics in the most prestigious English university, Oxford, from which Chairman Nzoka himself indirectly benefited a bit when he went to its Ruskin College institute many years back in search of improving his education before assuming a place in his nation's top leadership. Our Government didn't allow Tanzanian students to go abroad at government expense for courses which could be taken in the country, and Economics was certainly being offered at the University of Dar es Salaam. All the same it was decided that the request of the student Ndugu Mayala Nzoka Mwanakulanga was different and he was allowed to go and study Economics at Oxford on a full scholarship of the Government of Tanzania! Mayala's two immediate younger siblings, a boy and a girl, were studying in America at a most famous university in the fields of science and technology, MIT, with everything paid for by American missionaries of the Christian sect of African Inland Mission of Makongoro in Mwanza, great friends of his wife Bea. The other grown up children of Bea all passed and went to government secondary school at the end of the seventh grade of primary school, including those who were really dumb in class! With the children of Rose-Mary in Dar es Salaam, their mother had elected to send them to English medium primary schools right from the first grade. Her grown up children were in international secondary schools in Arusha and Moshi, and their younger siblings were at Dar es Salaam International School, all built especially for the children of rich white people in the country. As to the children of his white wife, the Kigamboni Beach Professor of Economics, and those of his Indian wife in Upanga and Zainabu Mary-Rose's child in Sinza, those who were still at home or were at nursery schools had two nannies each, and those going to nursery schools were driven to school in cars which had been bought especially for serving each child! Even his five children outside his marriages, as well as their mothers, had no worry in this world. Each one of those children too had a house built for him or her and a car bought to serve him or her, and their mothers were looked after by Mzee as if they were his real wives, as long as they continued to recognize Chairman Nzoka as their master, by remaining unmarried. And there wasn't a single one of them who had dared to even think of getting married to another man after having a child with Mzee.

Ndugu Executive Chairman Colonel Alhaji Muhamedi Nzoka Mwanakulanga had therefore every right to congratulate himself with *Alhamdulillahi!*

CONCLUSION

"A *ujamaa* nation can only be built by *wananchi* themselves, especially *wazalendo*," Mwalimu Nyerere repeated again, for the umpteenth time, at his last public rally for *wananchi* of Manzese. "Leaders are merely your servants. That is why the Party cannot emphasize often enough that rank is a surety-bond. Each and every leader, from a Ten-House Cell Deputy to me the President of your Republic, is a servant of *wananchi* to whom the people had entrusted that rank. It is true he or she is a leader, since the work of many people to be done well needs a leader. But the real builders of our nation are you *wananchi* yourselves, especially *wazalendo*."

That Monday Mwalimu had come to say good-bye to *wananchi* of Manzese before continuing with his tour of saying good-bye to *wananchi* in the whole country. After being President of the country for more than twenty years, Mwalimu had decided that time had come for him to step down, and he wanted to hand over the leadership of the nation to a new leader the people will choose. It would then be time for him to go back to his native village of Butiama and become an ordinary citizen like other *wananchi*.

He was surrounded on the platform by numerous Government and Party leaders, national, regional and district officials. Among them, and right close to Mwalimu on his right, was seated his trusted and dedicated servant and disciple of since the days of the struggle for independence, Executive Chairman General Alhaji Muhamedi Nzoka Mwanakulanga.

Nzoka now was no longer just a colonel. Sometime back on two or three occasions some monstrous creatures within the Tanzania *Wananchi* Army, consumed with greed for power and the desire for amassing wealth, had wanted to overthrow the legitimate Government of *wananchi* of Tanzania when their plots were discovered. And the person who unmasked their plots was none other than Ndugu Nzoka. As a result he was promoted with acceleration, skipping a lot of senior ranks on the way. First he was made Brigadier General and, shortly after that, a full General. Nationally too Ndugu Nzoka had climbed higher up the leadership ladder. In the last Party elections Ndugu Nzoka campaigned for and was elected Member of the National Executive Committee of the Party, and after that he was elected to the Central Committee of the Party by an overwhelming majority of his fellow members of the National Executive Committee. And during the general elections of 1985 he was elected by almost all the members of the National Assembly eligible to vote, the representatives of electoral districts, a National Member of the National Assembly as a candidate of the Youth League of CCM Party, the Revolutionary Party which had succeeded TANU at the helm of Tanzania's one-party society. Mwalimu, just before starting his tour of saying good-bye to *wananchi* of Tanzania as their President, had appointed Ndugu Nzoka as the Chairman of the National Committee for Operation Toilers Project. In order to help the more than 25,000 people who, like Saidi son of Jabiri, had been affected by the laying off of workers by the Government and public corporations in an effort to reduce costs, Mwalimu had directed *wananchi*, in spite of their poverty and the difficulties of their lives, to empathize with *wananchi* who had been laid off and contribute money to a Special Fund to help them help themselves while contributing to the growth of the national economy instead of staying idle. The campaign for raising money for the Special Fund was launched under the name of Operation Toilers Project, and Mwalimu entrusted into the hands of his faithful servant, Ndugu Nzoka, the responsibility of fund-raising as well as planning how the money raised would be utilized to make sure it benefited all the targeted *wananchi*. And immediately after the announcement of his appointment to that new responsibility, the National Committee for the Festivities of Saying Good-bye to Mwalimu on its inaugural session also elected him to yet another new responsibility of supervising the preparations of the festivities as their committee's Chairman.

Ndugu Executive Chairman Nzoka was therefore seated on the platform as a leader with many hats indeed, a dignitary who deserved sitting under the armpit of Mwalimu Nyerere that way.

Among the hundreds of thousands of *wananchi* of Manzese, Magomeni, Kinondoni, and elsewhere gathered at the rally to say good-bye to their beloved President that Monday afternoon was Ndugu Saidi son of Jabiri. That rally for saying good-bye to President Nyerere was more important to him than it could possibly be to any other person there. That day his wife Chiku had spent the last cent of the last salary he had received when he was retired from his work in the interest of the public of his nation, which he had served with dedication almost his entire life. How he would live after that, Ndugu Saidi saw nothing but absolute darkness on every side! Behind him it was all dark, where he was at the moment, again nothing but darkness, and ahead of him an even greater darkness loomed! Some years back the Government had conceived the idea of taking unemployed urban dwellers like him back to the villages. However in no time it became obvious that those have-nots, even those who had volunteered to go to the villages, couldn't cope with peasant life to which they were not accustomed. To them the life of wilding a hand-hoe while living in huts in the middle of the wilderness was not life but an insufferable jail sentence. Even those who had been toiling on really tough work in the city, like the coolies in the docks and laborers in other backbreaking jobs, did not find tilling land with a hand-hoe in the village to be life worth living but a jail sentence with hard labor! And in no time almost all of them had flocked back to the city and the other towns they came from. And even those who were determined to stay in no time realized that those villages had no economic foundation capable of giving them a new and better life than the life of misery they had in the towns. As a result by that year of 1985 there wasn't a single national politician and leader or anybody else in the country who talked anymore of "Operation Urban-Villages". What was more, peasants in villages all over the country were living under poverty and wretchedness just like the urban have-nots. Villagers everywhere had become dependent on food aid from the Government without which they would starve to death! And for years now Ndugu Saidi was seeing with his own eyes throngs of people flocking into the city from rural areas all over the country, as if urban life was any better!

When Ndugu Saidi and his son were retired from their work in the public interest, his son was still counted a temporary worker at their corporation. He was therefore not entitled to terminal benefits like the longtime and permanent workers who were retired with him. But, as it happened, Saidi himself, even though he had worked for the corporation longer than any of the other workers who were retired when their corporation took that cost-reduction step, was also retired without any terminal benefits. From what he was told, when he moved to the corporation from *Ikulu* he didn't take the steps necessary to make his transfer permanent as he should have done after working there for some time. Consequently, all those years he worked for the corporation he was on a temporary transfer! That was why he used to receive his entire salary without any contribution to his employee's benefits being deducted. And because he didn't contribute to his employee's benefits at the corporation, and likewise while he worked in *Ikulu* and at the Party Headquarters where he came from originally, he had no terminal benefits or bonus of any kind due him on retirement. What he got when he was retired was therefore only a table clock, a small radio and an ebony walking stick, presents from his fellow employees to their messenger, everybody's beloved *mzee* of so many years, and one month's salary!

That Monday therefore Saidi had decided to go for help to the only place left for him to seek help from: to Mwalimu Nyerere, his Mzee he began working for when he was still a little boy, his leader who knew his patriotism and his dedication to duty, the father of his nation full of compassion for the weak, the only person capable of seeing him with his problems as a human being worth helping. Mwalimu was retiring from his position, and therefore that was his last opportunity to appeal to him for help for his problems! Mwalimu was not a leader who could forget a person deserving his help. That was the decision Saidi arrived at after many nights of all-night long discussions with his beloved life companion, his wife Chiku.

He had arrived at the place where the rally was to take place really early: long before people eager to listen to their leader saying good-bye to them began pouring in. And that was exactly what he wanted. He had intended to arrive there early so that he could sit as near as possible to the dignitaries' platform. As soon as he arrived he sat down on the ground, all alone, in the hot Dar es Salaam overhead sun of one o'clock in the afternoon, and nicely folded his legs under him like a visitor seated on a floor mat in his hosts' house, when technicians were just beginning to set up loudspeakers on the platform. He was holding the table clock in one hand and the small radio and the ebony walking stick in the other hand, with everything placed on his lap as if he was cradling a child. The technicians at work on the platform looked at him in amazement! A crowd of children from the streets of the neighboring *Uswahilini* districts surrounded him wondering what was wrong with that *mzee*! Ndugu Saidi was however oblivious to all that. Even when and how people began to flock to the rally ground until it was full, when and how the dignitaries arrived and finally Mwalimu himself came and climbed onto the platform and that huge crowd of people split the sky with ululations and cries of joy and songs of happiness and of praise for their leader and his party and government were things which happened around him while his mind was completely absorbed with only one thing: how to communicate to Mwalimu his problems. Even what his leader and Mzee he respected and loved and trusted so much was saying were just sounds he heard and not words whose meaning he was following.

"Dear *wananchi* and fellow sons and daughters of our CCM Party, you have heard all I had to say to you! And you already knew it all since a long time. So let me also say good-bye with my same old message to you. The builders of a nation are its *wananchi*, especially *wazalendo*. Therefore, dear *wananchi*, we need to be *wazalendo* so that we can build..." On hearing that Ndugu Saidi was jolted out of his contemplations and realized that Mwalimu was concluding his speech and was about to leave the platform! And there and then he found himself already on the platform and giving Mwalimu his clock and radio and walking stick while saying, " Mwalimu, I am your former young man Saidi son of Jabiri of since the days of the struggle for our independence. Look at how I too have become an old man, with a head all grey just like you! I was recently retired from work and this tiny radio and this clock and walking stick are all I got after spending my entire life in the service of our nation!"

Nobody had anticipated what Ndugu Saidi did, and that was why not a single person in the President's security service was alert in time to prevent him from climbing onto the platform. What was more, Mwalimu had called the rally to say good-bye to *wananchi*, and it was quite possible that man saying good-bye to Mwalimu that way had been arranged by the organizers of the rally. Fortunately Mwalimu too still remembered very well indeed his former employee. Moreover, encountering people in that unexpected way had become for him the usual thing for very many years, ever since he became the beloved leader and father of the nation for *wananchi* of Tanzania. Mwalimu, therefore, without the slightest sign of surprise or concern, received the clock and radio and ebony walking stick and handed everything over to Chairman Nzoka right close by his side, just as he had done with the numerous presents the organizers of the rally had given him on behalf of *wananchi* of Manzese and elsewhere. In spite of that, it was still obvious Mwalimu had not understood very well the meaning of what Ndugu Saidi said to him when giving him those presents of his! Chairman Nzoka at once saw that Mwalimu was a bit disturbed and therefore hastened to put him at ease before his former fellow TANU Party faithful ruined matters on that public rally which was being broadcast live to the whole nation by Radio Tanzania. He whispered into Mwalimu's ear: "It is your messenger Saidi Jabiri I moved from *Ikulu* and appointed Head Messenger of our Corporation. He is giving you as presents the very presents he himself was given by the Corporation for being the best and longest serving employee when he requested to retire due to age and health problems." As soon as Mwalimu understood, the Father of our nation held the microphone firmly by one hand and then put an arm around Saidi's shoulders and drew him to him so that they stood linked shoulder to shoulder on the platform. Photographers from the national and international press at once flashed their cameras relentlessly, before Mwalimu had even uttered a single word.

"Ndugu *wananchi* and sons and daughters of our CCM Party, I had finished saying the few words I had for you, but I must add this one. This Ndugu here with his head all grey like me is an example of *mzalendo*. This Ndugu, Saidi son of Jabiri, is *mwananchi* who has served his party and his country and nation his entire life. When our party which fought for our *Uhuru* was still weak, without money or anything else, without rank to give to anybody, this *ndugu* joined the Party and worked for it as a volunteer, without any kind of pay! And my witness is none other than your leader with me here, Ndugu Nzoka, a great friend of his of many years with whom he was working for the Party. At least Ndugu Nzoka and my other assistants at the Party Headquarters were employees with a bit of pay, however miserable it was. Saidi on his part was serving his Party just as a volunteer, without any pay at all, and for a very long time. And even when eventually he became a paid employee, he still continued to do a lot of voluntary work for the Party for which he was not paid a penny! And Ndugu Saidi could not have had any ulterior motive for volunteering, because he was a simple messenger, a worker with no rank in the office and without any hope of occupying a high position in the Party. And Ndugu Saidi continued to serve his nation with that patriotic spirit his entire life, until he finally retired! And now here he is, in front of you, having come to give me, the leader of his Party, as his good-bye presents to me the presents he received from his work-place when he retired!" On hearing that Ndugu Nzoka decided to give back to Mwalimu Ndugu Saidi's presents so that he could hold them and show them to the sea of *wanamchi* at the rally. And Mwalimu lifted high the presents with his two hands. And the press photographers went to work with their cameras again, while the Radio Tanzania announcer informed the whole nation of what was happening there passionately and without pause as if he was announcing a soccer match between Yanga and Simba.[56] Mwalimu concluded the few words he wanted to add by handing back Ndugu Messenger Saidi son of Jabiri's presents to Ndugu Executive Chairman General Alhaji Muhamedi Nzoka Mwamakulanga. He did not sit down again or give his faithful follower of so many years the opportunity to explain further his problems to him. Without even waiting for his hosts at the rally to say a few words of thanks to him, the President of *wananchi* of Tanzania who was about to retire descended from the platform and got on his way back home to get ready to continue with his tour of saying good-bye to the rest of *wananchi* of our nation in the country.

The following day *wananchi* of Tanzania who had not listened to the national radio at the time of the rally or during the evening news heard broadcast on Radio Tanzania and read in both the papers of our nation, the Party paper in Swahili and the Government one in English, the news of the patriotism of Ndugu Saidi son of Jabiri. The two papers had on the front page the photograph of Mwalimu linked shoulder to shoulder with another old man with grey hair like him, Saidi son of Jabiri, with the same title in huge bold letters saying: "MWALIMU PRAISES THE PATRIOTISM OF A MESSENGER," a title under which Radio Tanzania too announced the news. And then the papers and the radio repeated what Mwalimu had said about Ndugu Saidi at the rally, to which they added a few words.

The Party had completed building for Mwalimu Nyerere in his native village of Butiama a place fit for the retirement of the first President of our Nation, a token of appreciation by the Party and the Nation for his great leadership which won us our Independence and built our nation for a whole generation. And at his residence in the village where he was born and where he intended to live on retirement the Government had build a Museum in which to keep the memorabilia of his historic leadership. The greater part of the Museum was especially intended for the presents of all kinds Mwalimu had ever received from *wananchi* of Tanzania: the traditional dresses of our different ethnic groups, bows and arrows and spears of our warriors of yore, togas and costumes of leopard and lion skins and crowns and headgears of all kinds our traditional rulers used to wear, and innumerable other presents *wananchi* from every part of our country had given Mwalimu from *Uhuru* to that year of

169

1985. In the news on the radio and in our two newspapers' coverage of Ndugu Saidi, the Chairman of National Committee for the Festivities of Saying Good-bye to Mwalimu Julius Kambarage Nyerere, the first President of the United Republic of Tanzania, was being quoted as adding to what Mwalimu said about Ndugu Mzee Saidi son of Jabiri by informing the nation that his Committee had decided to recognize the patriotism of that *mwananchi* by allocating the presents he gave Mwalimu a place among the select good-bye presents *wananchi* had given our first President and the Father of our Nation which would be kept in the Museum of the Leadership of Mwalimu in his native village of Butiama.

That was the additional news the people of Tanzania were told regarding how that *mwananchi* and *mzalendo* said good-bye to his great leader, the light of his life, the father of his Nation. That was how the difficulties facing the life of Ndugu Saidi son of Jabiri were addressed by the leaders of his *ujamaa* society.

NOTES

[1] Ndugu: Swahili for a brother or sister, and, by extension, any blood relative, a term by which Tanzanians called each other during the country's Ujamaa (socialist) era, the equivalent of "comrade" in socialist and communist countries at the time.

[2] Mzee: Swahili for "old man or woman", term of respect for an elder, and, by extension, ones superiors.

[3] Alhamdulillahi! Swahili (from Arabic) for "Praised be God!"

[4] A period of 40 days of observance after the burial of a dead person according to Moslem tradition. Increasingly, the period is now observed by non-Moslem Tanzanians as well.

[5] Bwana: Swahili for "Master" or "Boss", and also "Mr."

[6] Tumbo : Swahili for "Tummy", stomach, hence "Tumbo tumbo" emphatic repetition for "Big Tummy"

[7] Mnyapara Mkuu: Mnyapara is Swahili for "foreman and regulation-enforcer", especially during the colonial days. Mkuu is Swahili for "a great person" and, when used with a job title, "head" or "chief".

[8] Munubi: Swahili for "Sudanese", from Nubian.

[9] Mkosakabila: Swahili for "a person with no ethnicity", which usually connotes a rootless person who does not respect other people's social values, here human fellowship.

[10] Mwene: Title of a dignitary among Wamakua people.

[11] TANU: Tanganyika African National Union, the political party founded in 1954 by Julius Kambarage Nyerere, under which Tanganyika gained its independence in 1961.

[12] Uhuru: Swahili for "independence" and "freedom"; hence Tanganyika-huru for "independent Tanganyika" or "post-independence Tanganyika".

[13] Mwananchi" (plural "wananchi"), Swahili for "child of the land", usually meaning a black Tanzanian, and, by extension, an African.

[14] Mswahili (plural Waswahili): Informal Swahili for a black Tanzanian, and, by extension, an African; also a person of Swahili ethnicity, which is its original meaning, now used only in scholarly works.

[15] Mzalendo (plural wazalendo): Swahili for a "true patriot" or "die-hard patriot"..

[16] Ikulu: State House, Swahili borrowing of a Kisukuma word for the "king's palace".

[17] India town, "Uhindini" in Swahili: the commercial center of Dar es Salaam where Indians (which in Tanzania and the rest of East Africa usually means people of Indian, Pakistani and Bangladesh origin) had their shops and where they lived.

[18] Uswahilini: Swahili-town, the city districts where Waswahili or the Africans live, connoting the poor districts.

[19] Ujamaa: "Extended-family" socialism of one-Party Tanzania (1967-1985). The Swahili word "ujamaa" means "blood relationship."

[20] Mwalimu: Swahili for "teacher", the popular title of President Nyerere, the first president of Tanzania and father of the nation.

[21] Ugali: Swahili for a dish, nicknamed "stiff porridge" by the British during the colonial period, made by cooking flour in hot water, the staple meal of most Tanzanians, eaten with meat, fish, greens, beans or peas as relish. Different varieties of the food are found practically all over Black Africa.

[22] Genge: Popular Swahili term for a vending stall, especially one comprising a simple shed or sheds.

[23] Vizito (singular kizito): Swahili for "Heavy Weights", men of great wealth and social status.

[24] Degedege: Swahili for convulsions in children with fever, commonly believed to become fatal if treated with European medicines, especially injections.

[25] Banda: Swahili for a shed or simple four-sided building.

[26] Bibi: Swahili for "grandmother", also "Mrs." and "mistress".

[27] Babu: Swahili for grandfather.

[28] Mdogo: Swahili for "Younger" or "Junior", from "dogo" meaning "small"; hence "dogodogo", an emphatic form of "dogo" to mean "smallish" or "tiny", and, when applied to girls or women "tiny and pretty" and also "spring chicken".

[29] Mama mkubwa in Swahili. In Tanzania, and many other African countries, the sister of one's mother is either senior or junior mother and not "aunt", a term which is exclusively used for the sister of the father. Likewise the brother of ones father is senior or junior father, and uncle refers to the brother of the one's mother only.

[30] Kauzu: Swahili informal name for dry sardines (usually called "dagaa"), especially the very tiny ones from Lake Tanganyika.

[31] Kuruka: Swahili for "to jump" and "to fly", hence *kuruka* prices for "exorbitant" or "hiked" prices.

[32] Yanga: Short in Swahili for "Young Africans", a famous soccer team in Dar es Salaam, whose jerseys are yellow in color, and hence the popular Swahili word "yanga" for "yellow". Yellow corn is not grown in Tanzania and was brought in the country as famine relief foreign aid, mostly from the USA, and was considered not as good as white corn and food for the really needy people only.

[33] Kaya: household or home, Swahili borrowing from Kisukuma.

[34] Leaders: In Tanzania during the *Ujamaa* era (1967-1985) a leader was anybody holding a high ranking job or position in the party, civil service or public corporation.

[35] Id el fitr: The Moslem holiday at the end of Ramadan, the month of fasting.

[36] Kanga: A very light colorful cotton piece of cloth, usually with catch Swahili phrases written at the bottom, a pair of which women wear wrapped around their body.

[37] Vitenge (singular kitenge): heavy colorful cotton prints women wear wrapped around their body or make dresses with.

[38] Mitumba (singular mtumba): Used clothes, and, by extension, any used goods. The original meaning of the word is a "bundle" of something, and was applied to used clothes, which appeared first as an import in the country in the early 1980s, most probably because they are imported in bales.

[39] Kandambili: literally Swahili for "two strips", rubber flipflops, the footwear of the poor masses of Tanzania.

[40] Katambuga: Swahili phrase for "cut across grasslands", name of slippers made from old tires, probably to emphasize their durability.

[41] Aisee! Swahili from the English "I say!"

[42] Tabu: Common Swahili name for women which means "Problems". or "difficulties" in life. Hence Idaya's cynical punning.

[43] The education system Tanzania inherited from the colonial period ran from standard (grade) 1 to 12, with 1 to 4 as primary school, 5 to 8 middle school, and 9 to 12 secondary school. and 13 and 14 college preparatory grades. During the *ujamaa* era primary school was extended to run from 1 to 7 and grade 8 was dropped, and the four years of secondary school now ran from Form I to IV, with Form V and VI as college preparatory grades.

[44] Our white and Arab men: informal Swahili for "our rich African lovers".

172

[45] Konyagi: A Tanzanian made liquor.

[46] Naizesheni, Swahili borrowing of "Africanization", the replacing of white colonial civil servants and other foreign officers with Africans after independence.

[47] Baba: Swahili for father. When a married couple gets children, they call each other and are called by others as Baba or Mama "Father" or "Mother") of their first born, Baba Mayala and Mama Mayala, for example, for Nzoka and his wife Bea.

[48] Saba Saba: Swahili for Seven Seven, the 7th of July, the holiday for commemorating the founding of TANU Party on the 7th of July, 1954. The holiday has been retained even in multiparty party Tanzania, except nowadays it is celebrated as *Wakulima* Day, Peasants Day.

[49] Mgambo: Swahili for a public call to duty. *Jeshi la Mgambo*, *Mgambo* army, was a people's militia formed in Tanzania in the wake of the military coup which brought the dictator Idi Amin to power in Uganda at the beginning of the 1970s.

[50] Mchaka Mchaka: Swahili for "jogging", from joggers chanting repeatedly the words "mchaka mchaka" to keep pace with each other and boost their energy.

[51] Taarabu: Music of the coastal area of East Africa with a very strong oriental flavor.

[52] Mlimani: Swahili for "on the Mountain", reference to the University of Dar es Salaam, which is built on a hill.

[53] Imara: Swahili for "Firm" or "indestructible", also "resolute".

[54] Bubu: Swahili for "mute" or "silent", which in popular Swahili in business means lucrative business on the sly and illegal..

[55] CCM, Chama Cha Mapinduzi: Swahili for "The Revolutionary Party", the party formed when TANU of mainland Tanzania merged with the Afro-Shirazi Party of Zanzibar.

[56] Simba: Swahili for "Lion", the name of a famous soccer team in Dar es Salaam, the traditional rival of Yanga above.